VERY LIKE A WHALE

VERY LIKE A WHALE

Val Mulkerns

JOHN MURRAY

© Val Mulkerns 1986

First published 1986
by John Murray (Publishers) Ltd
50 Albemarle Street, London WIX 4BD

Typeset by Inforum Ltd, Portsmouth
Printed and bound in Great Britain
by The Bath Press, Avon

British Library CIP data
Mulkerns, Val
Very like a whale.
I. Title
823'.914[F]   PR6063.U378
ISBN 0-7195-4329-0

For

Maurice, Maev, Conor and Myles
who are home
but also for

Mary and Bernard
who have created a rather quieter second home
at the Tyrone Guthrie Centre, Annaghmakerrig,
where this book was written

HAMLET:	Do you see yonder cloud that's almost in shape of a camel?
POLONIUS:	By the Mass and 'tis like a camel indeed.
HAM:	Me thinks it is like a weasel.
POL:	It is backed like a weasel.
HAM:	Or like a whale?
POL:	Very like a whale!

I

It had never before been a problem which of them to visit first because they had been together every other time. Every other time he had got off the boat, hoisted up his rucksack, and walked with the straggle of travellers to where familiar faces were waiting behind the barrier. She would usually see him first and wave childishly with both hands and fingers spread. His father would stand smiling behind her, a head taller, one hand on her shoulder. They had met him together like that at the school train or coming home by plane from exchange holidays or at the boat after working spells abroad, like this one. But this one had lasted four years. He would not be met today because they didn't know he was coming home, and anyhow four years is quite long enough for things to change. 'But the change', she had written, 'is only superficial. You'll see, Benjamin.'

In the chill of the March morning, Ben hoisted his rucksack and grinned at the memory of that. A fantasist, as ever. Perhaps he would visit her first, and that meant unharnessing himself from his rucksack. The travellers he had watched getting jarred on duty-free booze and later giving it all back to the sea, flowed on without him to the waiting barriers, cleaned up now, and busily claiming their people. He looked back at the heaving sea and up at the familiar sunny spires before rummaging for the notebook. She lived not too far away, at Monkstown 'in a house that has been waiting for me all my life Ben'. Ah yes.

'Ben!' She had been caught as he knew she hated to be caught, wearing her oldest denims and a shirt covered in paint stains. It was, after all, March, the time she had always looked around for something to change even if it was only the colour of a room. But her welcome was real enough. She hugged him in the way that used to embarrass him as a schoolboy and that, even now, amused and touched him. 'Ben! Without a word to us, walking in like this out of the world. Come in. But maybe I knew in my bones you were coming all the same. Why else was *this* the day I got dressed in my oldest rags for finishing the job on the spare room? Only one door left to do. Come and let me look at you.'

'Hello Mother!' He examined her carefully too and saw that she'd never look young again as she still did four years ago. Her eyes were the colour of a blue shirt washed too often and her skin, though brown still from last summer, was papery at long last, like the hands holding his face.

She gave him breakfast in a room with yellow curtains whose window had hanging plants and a distant prospect of Howth Head. For him she had cooked eggs and bacon and predictably for herself had assembled a collection of nuts and fruit. As they talked she kept offering him morsels on his plate, as though he were a child still and not twenty-seven. She promised to bake wholemeal bread later that day.

'It seems selfish to go to all the bother baking for oneself, but I'll enjoy doing it today,' she assured him, and then quite suddenly, before he got out his own question, she began to tell him about his father. She might have been talking about a stranger of whom she was quite fond. As she spoke he looked around the room which was now full of filtered sunshine. The old walnut chest used to be in the back hall at home. The hanging bookshelves used to be in the dining-room. A blue pottery jar now filled with daffodils used to be in the small side window through which he would look coming in from school to see if anybody was in. For the first time since his arrival he felt disturbed. The rooms and passages that were his home were now full of other people's furniture. Other people wrote at the head of their letters 34, Victoria Place. It had happened two years ago, but it had seemed quite unreal on paper. Now in this pleasant, strange room were the familiar pieces of furniture that gave reality to the break-up. He rolled a piece of fresh bread between his fingers, feeling it become sticky again like dough. His mother looked as she used to look when she was anxious to make amends after punishment. She had never punished anybody very seriously except his father.

'We don't by agreement see one another too often, Ben. One has to become accustomed to separation.' She paused, and he remembered from a letter of his sister's that she had experienced two separations in two years. The man with whom she had set up this flat had walked out after a year. Back to his wife, Alison had written. And quite suddenly he also wanted to escape from his mother, from this sunny room where she had welcomed him and fed him before starting to tell him about his father.

'When you go to see him, Ben, make sure there's enough food in the flat. I'm sure he must often forget to buy replacements. And check on his elbows for thinning patches, won't you, and tell me if that boggy brown sweater that he likes to live in is on its last legs. I could buy him another one for his birthday. Why are you laughing at me, Ben?' In a second she was laughing at herself, covering her face with both hands in a youthful gesture that he remembered. 'Oh, I know. It's bloody hard for you to understand. It was hard for him too. But I'm not going to try to explain it to you now, except to say that you can't switch off almost thirty years like a light. Ask him, Ben, would he like some cuttings of the Wandering Jew for his inside window-box. He admired that. And say he can have any number of spider plants if he wants them. They grow if you simply show them the soil, they never fail.'

'Have all the telephone lines in Dublin been cut Mother?'

'I told you, Ben, it's not as simple as all that. Having separated from him, I will *not* crowd him. He must be given the same chance I took to remake his own life for himself – can't you see that?'

'But it's two years ago.'

'He doesn't find change as easy as – as we do.'

That was cunning. She was reminding him that he had walked out of a perfectly good job as a junior maths teacher four years ago. He had reverted to being a footloose student again and packed his rucksack with a suddenness which had shocked everybody.

'I think I'll stay with him if he'll have me,' Ben said suddenly. 'You don't mind?'

'No,' she said quickly, 'not at all.' But he saw the shock in her face and he knew she had probably been planning to finish the remaining door of the spare room before lunchtime with fast-drying paint.

'Look Mother,' he said, 'I brought you something from Holland. Not a clogful of bulbs this time. Or even a boot of begonias.'

She laughed as he rummaged. The clog of crocuses had been his present to her the first year he went away to squat in a house in Delft at the age of eighteen. It was the year of Juliet (who was actually called Helen) when he had played Romeo consciously for the first and only time in his life. People who lived in the streets around the market used to leave out good unwanted household items for collection by the binmen. When they became aware that he scanned them carefully for salvage before the collection began, the neighbours started leaving a chair or a stool or a perfectly useable fridge or anything good on the postage-stamp of sandy cobblestones behind which Helen and he had lived like mice in a loaf. At night it was never quiet. The lap of canal water never stopped. In the next boarded-up room to theirs rats pattered peacefully until morning. Helen said that even the rats were clean in

Holland and he had had to stop her leaving out food. It all might have been a hundred years ago.

'Look,' he said, handing his mother the package, a roll like a poster wrapped in striped paper, but fatter than a poster and heavier. She held it smiling in her hands.

'A sausage,' she said.

'Not a sausage. Open it!'

'Oh no!' Smiling, in a closed way she had learned to do since her teeth became darker, she held up with delight the small sumptuous carpet, and then went over to spread it, Dutch style, on a small round table in the corner. It glowed away from the light and she looked at it with her back to him for what seemed like a long time. When she turned to hug him he was embarrassed to see her eyes were wet and the only thing to do was bluster. Yet he marvelled to remember that this present had been consciously chosen to please and wound her at the same time. She and Denis had spent their honeymoon in Holland.

'When you see Denis,' she said, blinking, 'tell him to come over here with you for your meal on Sunday evening at half-past seven. No, don't. It's not fair cashing in on your return.'

'Have you actually seen him since you moved out?'

'Once,' she said. 'He was turning over a coffee grinder in Switzer's wondering would he buy it. I wanted to tell him not to because he'd never use it, but I ran away. I have his telephone number. You can give him a ring from here if you like.'

'No. I want to walk in on him in the same way. I'll see you on Sunday if I don't phone you before then.'

'Couldn't you, couldn't you leave your heavy rucksack?'

He knew this for the strategy it was. She had always agreed to things and then plotted to reverse them and get her own way. He shook his head.

'But I'll take a shower and a shave if you'll let me. And

maybe an hour's sleep. I couldn't get a cabin coming over.'
This was a sop to her as well as a kindness to himself.

Immediately concerned, she began to fuss out a big, clean
bath towel and then she led him to the small grotto which was
more a jungle of trailing plants than a bathroom. Curtains of
them fell almost into the bath and others curled about the
shower attachment. She told him that the condensation was all
the watering they needed – all were soppy plants which loved
the heat. He lay in the scented water and looked up at them
imagining them getting drunk on his bath. This was more a
place for a bath than a shower. Later she came and sat on the
end of his bed to tell him about his sister.

He fell shamefully asleep as she enthused about her grandchildren and he was only vaguely aware of her closing the
bedroom door and of her footsteps fading along the passage.

2

Friday was a day Denis liked but not for the usual reason of a weekend beginning. He liked it because on Friday he balanced his fairly new domestic duties against his work, getting both off his hands at the same time to leave two days clear for enjoyment. He collected on his way home items from four different shops because he disliked supermarkets. He ignored people who told him he was wasting money, including the lady who came to clean his service flat on Friday evenings. She was called Mrs Hughes and she belonged to the new breed of domestic workers. She was collected in a mini van with half a dozen similar ladies by the firm of contract cleaners based in Tallaght and he had never seen her wearing an apron. Spruce and neatly turned out she arrived quite often at the same time as he did from work. She told him once that she *ought* to take the tidy flat-owners like himself in turn and share them with her fellow workers but she had volunteered to be responsible for this flat, leaving it to be understood it was not an easy job. She wanted him to know that if everybody was as fussy about his place as he was there mightn't be much work for any of them. She left a fragrance of sprayed-on wax behind her and shining wet tiles with sheets of newspaper left for him to walk on as he put away his groceries. This was a homely touch which reminded him of a lifetime passed under another roof. He remembered a different cleaning lady for each child since the first one gave notice when Alison was born. The new

13

woman was even nicer and she stayed for ten years, Mollie. Like Mrs Hughes, she didn't mind cats, and cats liked her. One of the pleasures of Fridays these days was coming home to find his two long-haired beauties sitting each on a clean newspaper waiting for him. Each had a quite distinct croak of welcome and Mrs Hughes said they were too witty was what they were. Perhaps, on reflection, cleaning ladies had not changed so much, merely their method of employment and the cleaning devices they used. Gone for ever were those white cotton mops which stayed wet for weeks after use.

Today Mrs Hughes was gone, but she had kindly left a note behind reminding him to cancel his bottle of milk for tomorrow morning. He smiled at this, realising with some satisfaction how little she really knew about his life. The cats were nosing around the bags of provisions and he lifted one of them in each arm before putting the food away. They ran along his arms which was a habit of theirs and met together on the back of his neck both purring loudly. They had learned this trick as kittens, and it became a device to make him sit down. He walked with them scarfed around his neck into the next room and allowed himself the brief pleasure of plumping into an armchair and sinking his fingers into the silky fur of two cats who were suddenly in a heap together on his lap, jockeying for the best position. Cats preferred the lap which women wearing skirts made for them, if they had the choice, but his pair settled for what he had to offer. Cats were pragmatists and he had learned from them. Don't look back. Take advantage of every pleasure the present can provide. *Carpe diem.*

'Come on,' he said to them, 'I have something for you.' Instantly business-like they flicked together off his lap their feathery tails fanning his face, one ginger and one grey. They followed closely on his heels as he went back to the kitchen and rummaged out their fish. They liked it lightly poached in milk with a knob of butter dissolved in it the instant before it was given to them. While he prepared the Friday feast they twined and re-twined themselves around his legs, almost tripping him at times, and their purring was the only sound he could hear. Yet all around him the little separate worlds in this expensive block of flats prepared also for Friday night, running baths, turning up the transistor radio above the sound, rattling the pots and pans from which dinner would emerge, carrying in bottles.

It was an ugly place, utterly functional, and at first he thought he couldn't live there. It was built for the enrichment of speculators in the ruins of a lovely old house he had known since childhood, a flower of early Victorian baroque surrounded by hand-cut stone walls and a beech wood. It had stood at the junction of two roads in Rathmines and generations of children had searched there for birds' nests in springtime and in autumn had thrown stones to knock down huge chestnuts growing against the back wall. Now the beech wood was a car park and the building which replaced the house was what the auctioneers described as 'in tasteful reproduction style to match this mellow old Dublin suburb'. In other words it echoed features of the original but all its proportions were wrong. The cheap brick from which it was made had bled some sort of white substance along the façade and on Mondays the forecourt was a ruin of burst refuse sacks which he often tidied up himself, wearing rubber gloves. But the place was comfortable, there were those women to clean it, and even maintenance men living on the premises, and there were no ghosts. He had resisted the temptation to carry old letters and the like from his home to this place and he had stopped kidding himself that the useful accumulation of a lifetime in potting sheds and out-houses could ever be of service again – to any of his family at any rate, or to himself. So he had sorted and burned and thrown out in tight sacks and given away or left behind for the purchaser most of that old life that was over now for better or worse. If Olivia could do it, he could. In some ways the two years since all that had happened seemed like a decade. Routines were already established here and even the cats knew it.

On Fridays he liked to give them a specially delicious meal because on Fridays their freedom was deliberately taken away from them. They were gently bundled into the brush cupboard (where, however, he had taken care to provide soft beds and a litter for them) and there they knew they had to stay until some unspecified hour of the following morning. At first they had protested but cats are pragmatists, he had reminded himself once again. They endured Friday night and Saturday morning in return for the devotion lavished on them for the other five days of the week.

After he had fed them they retired to his living-room for their last digestive communion with his sheepskin rug, while he put away the groceries. He knew where you could find the best wholemeal bread, the best paté, the best cheese and even the best cheesecake. He always felt sympathetically conscious of the difference between himself and the young flat-dwellers buying their thin slices of this and that, and he tried to commit the extravagance of a whole cheesecake on Fridays as unobtrusively as possible. Once he had cancelled the order with the understanding young lady assistant when it was discovered there was only one cheesecake left and two or three young people who were looking for their single slices would have to do without if he took the cake away. At his old boarding school in the country that sort of thing was known as 'offering it up' and it was supposed to be good for the soul. With him it had become a way of life. But what he would never offer up was the pleasure of keeping cats. Stratagems would have to suffice.

It was half-past seven when he opened the windows to banish the steam of his bath and it was a quarter to eight when his cats were consigned to the brush cupboard. He had laid the table, lit the candles in the yellowing dusk and put on a Haydn quartet before the bell rang. He pressed the button on the tape-recorder before opening the door. She would exclaim as usual over the elegance of his preparations, and that always touched him. He glanced in the hall mirror and removed a cat hair from his collar before opening the door. She would smell of shampoo and clean young skin when she kissed him, arms linked around his neck, hanging onto him for a moment the way a daughter might. She called him Honey Bear and there was no way he could stop her. He imagined the exact expression on her face while he opened the door. Instead he found his son, beaming at him in a slightly embarrassed way, the rucksack loosened at his feet.

'I knew I should have phoned you, Dad, but –' The shock of the moment sent Denis's heart lurching and falling and made his mouth suddenly dry. He recovered quickly by embracing the boy and he fancied that when they looked one another in the face at last his own features were much as usual.

'You look younger than when I went away,' his son said, slightly surprised, and a laugh was the only answer to that.

'You look older, Ben – at last.' Ben's childish appearance as a young schoolmaster had been a trial to everybody especially himself. Now he actually had a few grey hairs and small lines, on either side of his mouth. 'Come in, boy, come in.'

There were several things he thought of doing immediately as Ben's rucksack thumped onto the floor. He could make a rapid phone call, but then wouldn't she be on her way? He could invent an appointment in town in ten minutes. He could brazen the whole thing out with style, but what about Anita? Almost immediately the doorbell rang again and there she was, exactly as he had imagined except for the bunch of daffodils, and she was ready to twine her arms around him until he indicated the rucksack on the floor. By this time Ben had wandered into the living-room and would no doubt be staring in astonishment at the candles and the folded napkins for two. Anita summed up the situation with a rapidity he wouldn't have believed possible and then laid one finger on his lips. 'Let me do it,' she whispered, and there was Ben, his acquired years suddenly gone from him, assuring his father how briefly he had dropped in and how, since he was staying with his mother, he should be getting along.

'This is Anita Quinn,' his father said, gently. And then, 'My son Ben.' But she had hardly waited for this. She was shaking hands, seeing resemblances in a second, asking him if he knew people she knew in Amsterdam, in Cologne.

'Join us for dinner, Ben.' Denis suddenly knew what to do. 'I'll set another place.' Ben stopped protesting, but he was wary, not as much in command of the situation as she was.

'Could you get me a jug of water from the kitchen, Ben, while I find a vase for these?' she said, and Ben was once more saved from speech. By the time the Haydn quartet needed to be turned they had finished their drinks and a manageable conversation was in progress. By the time they had finished the special paté spread on the special brown bread, Denis knew that Ben was comparatively at ease because he was ranting just the same as in his student days about police power in Germany. He had worked there for three out of his four years abroad, and he was still angry about it.

'I can walk home here at any hour of the day or night and nobody bothers me,' he said. 'Do that in Düsseldorf or in Cologne and you have a police car tailing you in no time at all. You don't have to have a suspicious bulge in your pocket or look in any way dangerous. You must convince *them* that you are simply walking home from a party or from a girl's flat. They don't have to give *you* any reason for creeping up on you in the police car and challenging you to produce your papers.'

'You didn't read about our newish Criminal Justice Bill,' Anita told him. 'This probably isn't quite the Dublin you left.'

'It felt free and easy as soon as I stepped off the boat, though,' Ben said, and over his father's takeaway lasagne and red chianti he heard about the new Dublin mainly from Anita, who looked as pretty as though her best subject might be

18

flower arranging. The soaring crime rate was drug-related she said, and the North's overspill of political violence was less important as a cause of crime than unemployment. She was a social worker and she knew about living conditions in Dublin city that people who lived this side of the river wouldn't believe.

Denis sat back as his cheesecake was passed around and he looked in a detached yet pleased fashion at his young guests who had more in common with one another than with him. When he had made coffee and come back to the familiar smell of the cigarettes Ben rolled he knew he was a little further removed from them still. Anita might be knowledgeable about the drug problem, but she wouldn't relate it any more than Ben would to the tall, criminalised green plant growing on thousands of window-sills or to the occasional nut of resin that homing students carried back with them like a luckpenny. He wasn't so sure about any of this himself, but Ben's mother had taken a soft line on soft drugs and had frequently advised the young on the care of their pot plants. The whole subject confused and worried him as he watched his Friday night breaking to pieces in his hands. No knowing how it would end. Not that he wasn't delighted to see the boy home again looking well and happy. Not that he wouldn't welcome him to sleep on the studio couch of this very room. But these Fridays had become the pivot on which his whole week turned, and this one was now out of his hands. He put on another string quartet and wondered how the night would end and also how his cats were. The two young people seemed to be linked together by their own clouds of pungent smoke. He had lost track of the conversation but he heard words like Eindhoven and air filter and computerised criminal records and he brought his mind back with difficulty to Ben telling about a world that hadn't been created when he was that age.

'He was a fool as I said,' Ben went on. 'The air filter is the first place they look. And the man at the customs post found it immediately – a single little piddling marble of the stuff, that was all we could afford between the three of us. We were arrested and strip-searched and although they found nothing else – because we had nothing else – we were taken to jail for questioning and kept in separate cells overnight. Next morning we were photographed, finger-printed and taken to court. The judge accepted that the amount of resin was so small that it must have been for our own use, but we were all fined and we all left that little courthouse with computerised criminal records – that's the point.'

'Quite recently a fellow in Dublin was jailed for two years for possessing a small amount of cannabis and a Nigerian was merely deported for being in possession of a large amount of heroin,' Anita remembered. 'Our courts are unpredictable. I don't accept you're any more restricted in Germany. But is that why you're home?'

Ben looked down at the last of the Chianti in his glass. 'Does anybody ever know why he's home?' he said. Suddenly he got up from his cross-legged position on the carpet and said he must go. His mother lived an hour's walk away.

'I'd drive you,' Anita said quickly, 'but I've got a better idea.' She handed him a key from her bag. 'Why don't you sleep in my flat and go home in the morning? It's only around the corner. Come on, Ben.'

'Or stay here,' Denis said, half-heartedly since she seemed to be taking charge. They left together, and he wondered should he release the cats, or wait for half an hour or so. He had a fatalistic feeling she wouldn't be back. However, he had barely cleared away and set the place to rights again when she was back, shaking her head and laughing at him.

'He's sweet,' she said, 'but oh God, how glad I am he's gone! Come over here to me Honey Bear and don't look so worried. He understands perfectly – why wouldn't he at twenty-seven coming in from the big bad world? Himself and his computerised criminal record!' She unbuttoned his trousers with deft, delicious fingers in front of the fire and went burrowing as usual. Then she encouraged him to undress her and in no time they were pursuing on his bed the customary transports of Friday night.

'What would you *do*, Honey Bear, if one lovely summer's day in the woods we met something horrible – a huge cat for instance that was menacing me and howling most hideously?'

'Kill him of course,' said Denis according to custom, 'and then make you a pair of knickers from his skin.' And then she screamed according to custom and it was time to cut the preliminaries. Later she was hungry again, and went to fetch more cheesecake from the fridge. She came back worried.

'You've never lied to me Denis, and I *know* you wouldn't. But I have this creepy feeling of cats stronger than ever at the moment. Have those people in the next flat acquired *another* feline friend?'

'If so I haven't heard,' said Denis truthfully, and as she ate, he lifted up handfuls of her newly washed hair and let them fall warmly through his fingers. He loved her and recognised the miracle of her feeling for him, but he would be happy as always to unlock the brush cupboard tomorrow morning. The return of his son from Europe lay warmly too at the back of his mind, until he remembered the armfuls of rubbish that had been carted from the boy's room: rubbish to them, maybe, but perhaps treasures to Ben. He was glad he had gathered up a box of oddments, everything from old copybooks to motor bike pieces, for presentation to Ben on his return. Next time he would remember to hand it over to be taken home, but where now was 'home' for Ben? The question troubled him, and he remembered the old house with the sharpest regret he had felt since he sold it to divide the proceeds fairly with Olivia, as she wished.

3

Alison's house was one of a row of artisans' dwellings dating from the turn of the century but recently discovered by the young middle classes. It was sturdily built of brick and stone, and it faced the river Dodder only a few steps away from Ballsbridge. Where once plumbers and carpenters and coopers and bricklayers had reared huge families without benefit of a bathroom, rich young couples had moved happily in and set about building sun-rooms and patios and bathrooms and au pair rooms and conservatories and playrooms. Because so many of them were architects or engineers or advertising people it was all done in excellent taste, nothing vulgar, nothing that wasn't sure to be in perfect harmony with the character of the little houses. But it all meant that they were now removed for ever out of reach of the ordinary Dubliners for whom they had been built. Such Dubliners now lived miles away from their work in huge suburbs clawing out into the countryside, each with the population of a large town and a multiplicity of social problems. Alison, on the other hand, could walk easily to work for her advertising firm in Harcourt Street or wheel her children along the river bank when she was free or down to Baggot Street and back with her groceries slung from a net on the underside of the pram. Her husband was a junior partner in a firm of architects and was sometimes away, but Alison never felt isolated. The river splashed and broke over its weir within sight of her front gate and she knew most of her neighbours. Besides there was Monique, specially acquired a few weeks before the baby was born and said to be a treasure by the family who were unloading her. On this March morning Monique was weeping as usual into her coffee over a letter from Paris and stirring in spoonful after spoonful of sugar. Her dark and sulky face was blotched with tears and she had already been asked three times to bring in the milk. All she mumbled each time was 'Pardon' and unfortunately a pact had been made with her parents that no French was to be spoken to her nor was she to be allowed to tune into ORTF on her little transistor. They should never have agreed to this because it was patently impossible to enforce. When the phone rang Alison had already taken up the infant to feed and she called to Monique to answer it. Monique cried louder into her coffee and Alison understood her to say in her guttering accent du Midi (where her parents had come from) that it might be Philippe and she didn't want to speak to him if Madame didn't mind. Sighing, Alison left the child at her breast as she went out to the phone and picked it up with her disengaged hand. This was one of the days when she worked at home by agreement and Monique went to her English class. At least that was supposed to be the idea. They had decided to be scrupulously fair and leave the girl plenty of time for study, but you could only indicate to the horse where the water was. You couldn't make her drink, as they had discovered.

'Hello. Yes, I know. Mother phoned me. *Hello, Ben.* Welcome home. Yes you could, of course you could. Or if you like I could meet you in town this afternoon and buy you a drink. No, well if it's all that urgent come on over. But give me two hours to get a bit of work off my hands will you? Why don't you come over at 12.30 and have cheese and yoghurt or something with me. OK. And it's simply lovely to hear your voice again. 'Bye love. See you.'

Ben at the other end of the phone in a public call box smiled. If he'd told her he had a broken back and was waiting to be

23

released from a crashed car would she still ask to be given two hours? Probably only one hour. Still smiling he laid down the phone. Little sister Alison. On top of every situation since she was five years old. Her conveniently wild youth (like everybody else's) was fitted into neat little boxes. A few wild boy friends, including a Provisional IRA man, whom she wore like trophies around her neck and discarded when they grew too fond of her. At the same time people were thinking, 'Poor Alison, somebody should take her aside and tell her. The permissiveness of parents can go too far,' etc. Then there was the abortion neatly and successfully handled entirely by herself and known to very few outside the family. Even the family didn't hear until afterwards and then only because Alison was so pleased with herself. Then Canada and the beginning of this advertising thing, after she had changed direction twice at college before graduating. Home then to rapid success at her first job followed by marriage to the first really good prospect.

She was still only twenty-six, but she had two children and a devoted architect husband who would probably end up owning his firm. So Ben's mother had told him.

Ben walked down from the phone box to the little beach in the first mild sunshine of the year. He thought about Alison in this place where they had both played as children and an incident which he didn't remember but which his mother had related over and over again to make visitors laugh. Alison is three years old, with a head of golden curls and an angel's face. She is square and sturdy. A thin little boy six months younger is making a sandcastle with a heavy, functional spade which is a bit too big for him. Alison snatches this spade and leaves in its place an ineffectual wooden one which is all she is allowed to have herself for safety's sake. The child screams and manages to get his spade back from Alison who grabs it again and taps him lightly with it on the head and walks off. Her mother arrives to administer justice, removes the spade from Alison whose screams match those of the small boy. In no time at all the parents of this child are comforting Alison exclaiming over her charm, forcing their own child to play with the wooden spade and restoring his to Alison, whose tears turn off like a tap and who gives the boy's parents her angel smile in gratitude. The gods love Alison, but she will live to be a hundred all the same, Ben decided, rolling over on the dampest gritty sand from which a morning tide had ebbed.

With the mountains at his back and the silky bay at his feet his mind was not at ease. It was in Düsseldorf at the industrial plant under construction, and he was climbing the scaffolding, already so high that from the ground he knew he looked a blue speck with an orange helmet, an insect among other insects climbing and toshing. It didn't much matter how you got the paint on. You covered the spidery constructions with an anti-rust substance and the aim was to cover every inch of them. You incidentally at times covered every inch of your overalls and your shoes and your face and your helmet. In a high wind you had no alternative and the noise would probably waken him at 3 a.m. for the rest of his life. You didn't look down past the phalanx of steel to the insects on the ground below. A safety device should have been fitted to your belt, but in this sort of lumpwork organised by a crooked Irishman there were no inspections. An eighteen-year-old student had crashed to his death last year, having stayed up drinking too late the night before. Most of these insects clambering and toshing around him would be drunk tonight. They would find noise and heat in an Irish pub and only turn into the workers' hotel for five hours sleep before the morning call. No time for breakfast. Breakfast would be at 10.30 after three or four hours work. Lying on the familiar beach, known to him since childhood, he smelt the good coffee and heard the clamour all around him with which he had had to live, then he grinned and thought of Alison. He had been as well equipped as she for the soft life and he hadn't the excuse of artistic ambition to get out. A lonely impulse of delight, old man Yeats called it, but he meant something else. Ben had even had a school to teach in and a pay cheque coming in every month and he didn't even dislike teaching. He disliked the lives people made according to custom for themselves. He disliked nice houses where you had to remain, having hung them around your neck with the bank's blessing. He disliked the idea of paternity and fidelity and growing old faithfully among the neighbours who had also hung mortgages around their necks and signed their bawling newborns in for the best schools with the placid trust that they would grow up to attend them, which they probably would. He disliked even the suspicion that he might turn out to be like everybody else, like Alison who needed two hours to prepare for you to visit her.

He and Julie had been different. The flat in Düsseldorf had been like a shoebox, but there were always friends from Ireland sleeping on the floor and he had only been treacherous to them once. His mother was calling to see them on her way home from skiing with a new friend. He imagined her picking her way across the bodies on the floor and sniffing with incredulity the pong of old socks at five o'clock in the afternoon and he told them to go. Pointed them at a Youth hostel, threw their sleeping bags out on the landing, took a few days off from work at his own expense to clean the place up. Julie had been unnecessarily frightened of his mother and had stayed in bed, but their bed was up a narrow wooden ladder which led to a doll's room under the roof. Somebody had fitted a drawer for clothes under the divan and she had entombed herself in there with a handful of sleeping pills in case his mother should care to climb the ladder. His mother did comment tactfully on the convenience of it all, and did not lift the fringed shawl covering the drawer. The thing was all over in an hour and then she took him out to dinner with her new friend. Julie had been frighteningly hard to wake up when he got home. After that they had gone to live in Delft where she wanted to study painting but not to take any exams. Delft

26

began her long love affair with Vermeer and the end of her and Ben. But even the beginning of the end had been difficult and he didn't want to remember it. He wondered vaguely in the warm sunshine where she was and how she was. He recoiled from thinking specifically about her health problems as about her method of dealing with any difficulty by running away. Yet she had shared three out of four years of exile and he had never seen her before they had checked in on the same flight together. She had asked him to hold her hand at lift-off because she was terrified of flying. Among other things. Among everything. Julie was the sun but she was afraid of being burned, of being alone, of becoming pregnant, of waking up one day and finding she was old, of mastectomy, of examinations, of staying at home, of running away. He had ended up being afraid of her crushing, total dependency on him, but he didn't even want to think about that. Not this morning in the first sunshine of the year on this awful gritty little beach that he had dreamed of off and on for four years. When he closed his eyes abroad it was that house out on the point he saw, or Howth adrift ahead of him in mists, or the gold-topped spires of the parish church reflected in a full tide. He got up and walked around the point to the harbour and then it was time to think about walking to Alison's place. When Alison said twelve-thirty she meant it, not twelve or one o'clock, but it was too fine and pleasant a morning to think of anything but a walk. His first shock was to see the strange structures which replaced the vanished Victorian villas between Sandycove and Dun Laoire. They were a version of his father's apartment block but higher and dismayingly wrong in the context of the summer place. Car parks replaced gardens. The people he met seemed to have been imported with the architectural design, if they really were designed, that is, and not put together by the builder. He remembered suddenly seeing an old house being reconstructed in Amsterdam, dismantled brick by brick, each of which was numbered. In

27

Holland it was against the law to use new materials when listed houses had to be repaired. It was quite possible to repair or even extend the structure and replace the façade so that nobody could possibly tell the difference. In Dublin the destruction of the city's most typical buildings had begun of course long before he had gone away, but he hadn't been so conscious of it. Now he had the disturbing feeling that his own city had vanished during his absence and he hadn't even seen Stephen's Green yet. His mother had warned him about that. 'Don't expect to find your old Dandelion Market,' she had warned him.

At Booterstown, where a sky such as this one used to dazzle the white walls of the old Imco factory, there was a strange deadness of new concrete which seemed to absorb the March light and give nothing back. But birds still wheeled over the sloblands. He might spend an afternoon there. On second thoughts why not get down to the shoreline now and walk along to Sandymount. He turned sharply right at the Booterstown Avenue junction and made his way down to the soft ridged sands still sloppy from the morning tide, and dyed blue by the sky. Birds he could have identified with no bother as a schoolboy shovelled and picked around for their breakfast. One in fact was a shoveller, and further out he saw a redshank, but there were several other busy species that baffled him. Herring gulls, however, were not possible to mistake. They hung huge above the channel watching their chance of fish on the bone and then on a sighting they dropped like stones. As he watched them, his feet gently sinking into the sand, he saw a flash of silver as one of the gulls made a kill and instantly moved out with it away from the flock, no doubt to find a private rock for his feast. Ben became absorbed in the drama of survival and forgot the vague unease of the walk from Sandycove. His body felt light. He even had a return of the childhood fantasy that by lifting his arms like wings he could take off like the herring gulls and drift down at will by holding out his arms

28

motionless. The sun strengthened and he threw off his denim jacket and slung it over one shoulder. Then he resumed his walk towards Sandymount Tower which incorporated a kiosk where you could buy ice-cream when he was a child. At Sandymount he looked in disbelief at the oily black traceries which made a pattern all over the strand and piled up in sinister rolls along the tideline. Sewage or oil pollution? A present from Winscale renamed Sellafield? Who knew? It didn't smell of anything but rotten seaweed.

At the tower he went by St John's Road with its echoes of the lost Edwardian city back to the main road and on to Ballsbridge where again a huge office block, entirely empty in the sunshine, blotted out the sky over the river and dwarfed the houses in its monstrous shadow.

He was a little late when he reached Alison's house and she was waiting at the gate facing the river, a blonde little girl at one elbow.

'I was just wondering whether or not to begin,' she reproved him before rushing over to kiss him. He lifted up Olivia, named after her grandmother but looking exactly like the old photographs of Alison, and he carried her in under the carriage lamps to the most charming of doll's houses, all stripped pine and Laura Ashley prints with an old dresser and hanging shelves and a spicy smell of new bread in the kitchen. This room had been extended out into a cobbled yard to form a conservatory and a green light from dozens of hanging plants came in from there. A converted oil lamp hung among the plants and it would presumably be switched on at night. From a room upstairs came the incongruous sound of rock music.

'Let me look at you,' said Alison exactly as their mother had, and he put the child down and laid a hand on each of Alison's shoulders, bending down to stare at her. The face was plumper than he remembered and the dimples less obvious, but it would always be the face of a blonde child. It would not wear well.

'You're thinner,' Alison said, 'and you've a few wrinkles but they suit you.' Obviously feeling this a little inadequate after four years she hugged him again, and rubbed the top of her head against his chest in a remembered gesture. 'It's so lovely to see you again Benny. I've always read the letters you wrote to the parents yet I know I have never sent you more than an elegant postcard and even then it very probably arrived just the day after you left for some place else. Sit down.'

'I did get a few of them,' Ben said. 'Some of them are brightening somebody else's horizon on an attic wall in Eindhoven. I particularly liked The King's House, 65 The Close, Salisbury (John Buckler, 1807). It faced me on the wall when I lay in bed – its six golden gables and its twelve tall chimneys. Inside, the King is playing a madrigal and waiting for his current mistress to arrive. The grass is golden so it's flaming summer. Maybe the King is playing his madrigal in the arbour rather than indoors. Or maybe not.'

She examined him carefully and not unkindly as she rested her head on the head of the child who had scrambled up onto her lap.

'May I ask you why you did it Ben? Throw it all away I mean, and go off like a schoolboy again? You've no idea how the parents worried about you!'

'Don't be romantic Alison. Surely I gave them the opportunity to separate *kindly* since they weren't going to tumble the roof over my head?'

'Was that why you went?'

'No.' He laughed at the bizzare idea. 'No. I only wish I saw things as simply as you do, Alison.' Without speaking, the blonde child removed herself from her mother's lap and sat on his and Alison got up abruptly and began to slice the newly baked bread which she brought to the table. A bottle of white table wine from the fridge followed and she refused his help to open it. He was bidden to sit down to liver paté she had made herself, a salad of chopped fruit and nuts and the tossed green salad in a wooden bowl. There was another wooden bowl of

30

red apples on the table and a slice of Brie on a blue dish flanked by a small bunch of green grapes.

'Welcome home, Ben,' Alison said, toasting him in the sweetish but nicely chilled wine. She immediately excused herself and went to the foot of the pine staircase which spiralled up from a corner of the room.

'Come and have lunch with us, Monique?'

'Merci mais plus tard,' came the muffled response. The rock music had ceased and Alison came back shaking her head. She helped Olivia to a small portion of everything as she began to ask the child about play school, drawing her out for her uncle's benefit. Olivia attended a little play school around the corner run for the children of friends and neighbours by (he fancied) somebody very like Alison. Young Olivia looked smilingly down at her plate but didn't speak.

'If you eat up all that, I have something for you in my pocket,' Ben said, slipping easily into the customary way of speaking to children, much to his own surprise.

'Have you something for Alison too, Ben?' the child asked, and when he nodded the two blonde faces opposite him smiled together. Alison and he talked easily enough then of mutual friends and how each had fared. He learned of marriages and births, and sometimes births before marriages, and he also learned of some casual arrangements but there were fewer of these than he would have suspected, certainly fewer than there used to be when he went away. Alison spoke of them with the slightly patronising regret of the new Puritan. He wondered if he should mention the meal with his father but she saved him the trouble.

'He's making a fool of himself Ben – you've no idea! It's a miracle Mother hasn't picked up the story. The girl is a year or two younger than I am and a proper little tart from what one gathers. Colm thinks I should mind my own business but I'm not at all sure I shouldn't ask him over and talk to him. I mean, what could she possibly be after at his age but his money?'

31

Ben covered his face with his hands and shook his head.

'Have you forgotten so much about him?' he said at last. The stronger language which sprang more easily to his lips was suppressed because of the child. 'Your husband is right, Alison. Mind your own tidy, well-organised business and leave Dad to enjoy the rest of his life in *his* way. I've met her as a matter of fact and slept a night in her flat.'

'You've *what?*' his sister gasped, and he took pleasure from her confusion before explaining.

'I liked her and I think she's probably wonderful for him.'

'But think of how Mother would feel if she knew!' said Alison righteously. 'Only think.'

Ben smiled, watching the face of the child across the table from him with sudden pleasure. He remembered an old-fashioned great aunt and what she had said to his mother about the five-year-old Alison who had had to be punished one day for something outrageous. Aunt Georgina had said gently to his mother, 'Remember, my dear, small children are only on loan to us. Prize them. Love them. In ten years or less they'll be gone with all their magic and all their innocence. Don't waste time punishing them.' In ten years or less, thought Ben, that blossom across the table will be starting to be another Alison.

'Pas devant les enfants,' he said to the mother with a grin. 'But you're so bloody wrong, Alison. Think about it. Even at long distance I knew about Mother's Gregory.'

'She was a *victim*,' said Alison piously. 'Like so many women. And it lasted no time at all. How can you possibly compare the situations?'

'Don't let's quarrel over this delicious meal, Alison. Let me pour you more wine.'

'No thank you, I don't want to turn my son into an alcoholic. But pour yourself some.' She had hardly finished speaking when a baby's cry from upstairs sounded straight on cue, and presently a sulky French girl came downstairs carrying a bundle which she deposited on Alison's lap. Alison opened a few buttons and gave the child her breast with the casualness of long practice, making introductions at the same time.

'Enchanté,' the French girl said and instantly went back upstairs.

'Could you make the coffee please Monique,' Alison called after her, but Ben got up immediately.

'Would you let me make it?'

'She's lazy enough but if you like . . .'

'I'll show you,' his niece said sensibly, and he was delighted by this early hint of her practicality. She was perhaps an Alison already at four years old. On the way out he paused with some pleasure to watch the infant feeding, its total absorption in the job on hand.

'Just like a man about booze,' said Alison smugly. 'Look at him.'

In the kitchen beyond the alcove Olivia showed him where the coffee was and as he was arranging the filter she climbed on a pine stool at his elbow and whispered, 'I'd like my present now please Ben, if you don't mind.'

'Certainly,' said Ben. 'Just let me get this going.' Her present rummaged from his pocket found approval and she rushed in to show it to her mother. He could hear Alison exclaiming over it with delight and he was sorry he hadn't brought one for her too. What appeared to be a simple matchbox was in fact a miniature Dutch kitchen when you opened it: big stove with blue and white tiles and a seat surrounding it, copper pots and pans on the wall, blue and white checked tablecloth, a hanging lamp, and a woman with a Dutch bonnet and dogs at the stove and a ginger cat. It and many others of its kind had been made by a girl whose room was next door to his in Düsseldorf. She sold these things in the street market on Saturdays and he had another one in his rucksack. But not for Alison. When he came in with the coffee he gave her the silk scarf he had bought for her in Paris last year and she exclaimed politely over it, but all her attention was on the Dutch kitchen. He started to tell her

33

about the girl who made it as they drank their coffee.

'An artist obviously,' Alison said, moving the infant over to the other breast.

'A failed one, unfortunately. She worked as a translator of soft porn into German. Making these miniatures was her recreation. Ever since the day she sold one she was pestered by people for more.'

'Did she make a good living?'

'She made a lot of money but her living expenses were high. She used heroin.'

'Didn't you try to stop her?' Alison said horrified. 'That's what friends are for.'

'I didn't try to stop her. It wouldn't have been possible. She used heroin because her life was intolerable otherwise.'

'She was an addict of course?'

'I never really knew,' Ben said. 'According to herself she wasn't. But she's dead anyway.' Ingeborg Schnell where are you now? He suddenly found the beauty and cosiness of Alison's nest intolerable but he needn't have worried as his time was up.

'I'm due into work in half an hour and there's just time to walk down for exercise. Come with me?'

'Why not?'

He cleared away the table while Alison took the infant upstairs. His niece helped him in her own way.

'What was her name Ben, the girl who made my kitchen?'

'Her name was Ingeborg Schnell,' said Ben. 'Say it!'

The child's efforts to get her tongue around the name occupied the remaining time. Alison came briskly downstairs wearing a thick Aran gansey over her jeans. She scooped Olivia up in her arms.

'Say goodbye to Uncle Ben, love, and promise me to be a good girl when Monique takes you out for a walk?'

'Goodbye Ben,' Olivia said and when Alison passed her over he kissed the small, familiar face. 'See you again soon,' he said,

34

and set her down.

'I want to show Monique my matchbox,' Olivia said.
'Bye-bye Alison.'

'Will you be good for Monique?' But Olivia was already
vanishing around a bend of the stairs.

'She's going through a stage when Mama and Dada have
been shelved for the time being. I'm Alison and he's Colm
which we rather like but Mother says it won't last.'

'Nothing lasts,' said Ben cheerfully and as they left the doll's
house the sound of heavy rock music was turned up again.
Willows in a haze of young green were trailing into the river
opposite and as they walked along the banks in the direction of
Lansdowne Road she began to tell him about the heroin crisis
in Dublin. He remembered that three years ago a couple of
Dutch friends returning from Dublin predicted a worse problem soon among the very young than there was at that time in
Amsterdam. As they crossed under the dusky railway bridge
Alison brought up the subject of their father again and sug-
gested that Ben 'speak to him man to man'.

'You sound like somebody in an old-fashioned melodrama,
Alison. What do you suggest I say?'

'Oh anything that isn't too offensive about a truly *embarrassing* situation. If Colm's parents got to hear of it they'd
think we're a very odd family.

'We are a very odd family and this conversation is the oddest
thing about us. Goodbye little sister and thanks for the lunch.'

Before stepping on a bus he stood bemusedly to watch her
confident, chunky walk in the direction of town.

4

Beech Park,
Monkstown
March 16th
Phone 630777

Dear Julie,

It could have happened and I thought it would, and for a week I've been in and out of Dublin pubs and walking the streets in the fairly positive belief that some pub, some street would be the one. Where are you? Will they know at home where to send this? I looked for them in the phone book and I gather they are still resisting the idea of an electronic intruder in the house. In a way it's like putting a letter in a bottle and tossing it onto the tide but there you are. The mood is on me and I have to know how you are. Married perhaps and snug like Alison? Living with the perfect mate in unwedded bliss? Happy somewhere on your own in a flat the size of a matchbox because you hate open spaces? Travelling? An attic in Paris? A basement in Delft? An island house in Greece? Where are you? If I throw this into the sea at Sandycove will it find you? Or should I post it? If I do will it reach you and will you say 'Ben, Ben Who?' for the reason that since all those months ago you've known a plethora of Bens, Benjamins and Benedicts and Bernards, Bens to a man?

This Ben (who once knew how to write paragraphs) seeks an hour or two of your company to learn about your new fears and banish them for you if he can or to learn that you will never be afraid of anything again because you are a grown-up lady now with a baby like Alison, or rather, two babies like Alison. You may have forgotten by now but you met her once when she came visiting and she cut your hair for you and made you a nice new plan of living. Remember? She's the sister who can't fail to succeed and she's never tried very hard anyway. She's made me an uncle and I'm not ungrateful, somewhat charmed in fact by the small apple-cheeked creature who speaks like an adult but who nevertheless nearly failed to say Ingeborg Schnell. She was a sad junkie I knew in Düsseldorf and when I see you I'll tell you – nay, I'll show you – why a chunky little girl whose parents have created the perfect doll's house around her (with a river running past the door) spent five minutes in my company trying to get her tongue around Ingeborg Schnell. Oh Julie, phone me and don't just intend to if and when you get this. Switching off is not so easy when you have lived in somebody's pocket for two years as I have in yours and you in mine. It was necessary to break up but now it's time to see what time has made of us. But me no buts. Tell me where you can be found.

Je t'embrasse,

Auf wiedersehen,

Ben

He found it hard to believe he had been a week in Dublin and that this again was Friday – a day which he suspected to be *not* the right day to visit his father. He thought he could detect in last week the feeling of a weekly ritual – the candles, the carefully purchased components of a meal. All his life his father had been methodical and a teacher of method to others. Maybe all chartered accountants were like that. Ben had resisted being organised for most of his life at home. His room had been a monument to planned disorder. He liked for instance to put books in current use on the floor so that when he wanted to consult them all he had to do was flop down in the appropriate place. He had thrown out his wardrobe and put up six or seven wooden racks on the wall for his clothes, but they had only held clothes he didn't use any more. His current garments were usually on chairs or on his bed and he had his own highly unorthodox ironing method. Trousers were put between his bed frame and the mattress and other garments between the top sheet and the quilt so that the heat of his naked body would smooth them out. It used to be his gesture of independence, although self-reliance didn't go so far as washing his own clothes. It did dictate that he remove them independently from the family bundle and deal with them himself.

Now that his mother was living alone she had told him that it would be good for the machine to have a proper load and she had put a handsome wicker basket in his room and urged him to use it. But some streak of cussedness rather than independence caused him to gather up his bundle of washing today and make with it in his rucksack for the local launderette. It was too early for the weekend crowd and the girl out of boredom offered to attend to his bundle herself, if he liked, and he could call back later. When he returned there were three customers reading magazines in front of their whizzing machines and one of them was familiar, so familiar that the breath left his body for a moment and his legs weakened as he pulled a book out of his pocket to regain composure. She had not looked up. He had the sudden conviction that *she* was not reading either. Her copy of *Magill* was open but her eyes were not moving. She was thinner and weedier than she used to be, and her colour was unhealthy. He got the impression that this might be her only trip out of doors for several days. Her thin legs in grey tights were crossed and she wore grey suede pull-on boots with flat heels. Her voluminous (as ever) cotton skirt was grey too, but on top was the familiar flamboyance of the Mexican wool sweater which made her face seem paler when she looked up. There were blue blotches under her eyes. She hadn't been sleeping again. What he wanted was for her to discover him rather than the other way round, but she looked so locked into herself that he hardly thought this possible. On his way to collect his bundle he put a hand on her shoulder, and it too was thinner. When he smiled at her and bent to hug her as she looked up, he saw the withdrawal in her eyes, inky blue and very wary in the white face.

'Ben!' she said, and he supposed her pressed-together lips with the upward lift at the corners represented an attempt to smile.

He kissed her on the mouth and said, 'I wrote to you. I even posted it to the parents' house yesterday. You got it this morning?'

'No,' she said. 'No!'

'Where are you staying?'

'Not too far away but not here. This launderette is less crowded than where I live. How are you Ben?'

'I'm fine. You?'

'OK.'

'Come and have lunch with me in town after you've dropped home your bundle. Come up first with me while I drop mine. I'm staying with Mother at the moment but she's not in. We can have coffee anyway and we can talk. God, I'm so *glad* to see you, Julie. On the heels of that letter it's a sort of miracle when I've been looking for you for a week. I've a lot to tell you.'

'Yes,' she said. 'But I can't come into town with you, you know. I'm working this afternoon and anyhow I have an appointment that I can't break at lunchtime.'

'Couldn't you take me along too? I'm quite clean and respectable and I polished my shoes the day before yesterday.'

'No Ben,' she said, then, smiling for the first time, 'but I'll give you a ring, promise.'

She was sending him away, untalked to, and he was acutely aware of his misfortune in meeting her before she had got his letter. He scribbled his mother's phone number and address on the back of an envelope and he gave it to her. She looked down at it, smiling still, and put it away in one of the skirt pockets from which she would probably lose it. He felt a little frantic. A toss of the coin and he might have found a way to get through to her again.

'Can't I just –?'

'No Ben,' she said, with total composure as she picked up her magazine again. He touched her hand on the way out and it was cold, even in this warm, steamy place of rattling machines. But she winked slightly in a quick familiar flicker as a goodbye, and he had to accept that as a hope of seeing her again.

Outside in the cold March sunshine he walked briskly towards his mother's house and then didn't want to go in before he had come to some conclusion about Julie. Was she ill again? Under sedation for a pain that could become unbearable as he knew? In some sort of trouble? At war with the parents? Simply not interested in seeing him even in friendship again? Still angry because the decision to break up had not been hers? Impossible to tell, but on the whole he thought her health was the most likely trouble and that bothered him. Like everybody he'd ever known except Julie he took his own health for granted, but sometimes in nightmares he was in hospital again after the crash, his back in traction, entirely enveloped in pain, cut off by it as though by a wall at times, and at other times as though by a malevolent animal that slept and woke up too soon, anxious to get to grips with him again. He seemed to remember his parents constantly at his bedside. The doctors kept changing the dope they gave him, fearing addiction, and always before they changed to something else there were certain hours of several days when the effect wore off in half the time and he would lie there totally engulfed, pulsing with pain, cursing occasionally at passing nurses when they shook their heads and said they must see Sister before they could give him another injection. One of them was young and dark and calm with a nice smile and she would look him in the eyes a long time before deciding about him.

'We don't want to blitz your brain entirely, Ben. This stage will be over in another week and then you won't know yourself.'

'I won't live another week,' Ben would assure her, and then she'd give the smile again when she saw him grinding his teeth and rolling his head from side to side on the hard bed. No pillow of course.

Mostly she would call a nurse and issue another instruction and then for a few days the pain would be under control and the larkiest of the student nurses who was from Kerry would put her hand under the sheet and smooth the place closest to his limp penis and whisper to him, 'You'll not catch me doing this next week, Ben!' before she dodged quickly away at the sight of authority. He thought it was this girl who did most to bring him back to the land of the living because he wanted to surprise her and one day he did (but it was several weeks later). She went away giggling and soon after that he began to look around him in the Honda Ward.

He was told there was a ward like this in every hospital, full of surgical cases after motor bike crashes, and (like this one) mainly visited by fellows in leather knee boots and jackets carrying crash helmets who left them carefully down under the bed before turning to say hello. Sometimes it was like a party, especially when he recovered a bit. In this section of the hospital they were easy about visiting and Alison for instance often stayed all afternoon, sitting there eating his grapes and talking interminably about school when she should have been there. They attended the same co-educational establishment and he was supposed to do special work once he grew better and give it to Alison to bring in. But he did no work. He drew breath and savoured the absence of pain. He did crossword puzzles and mathematical teasers and he read *The Financial Times* and he was promised rapid progress once he was well enough to get into the hands of a physiotherapist. Then the pain began all over again, worse at times than the earlier stage, when effects were more to make his spine flexible again and to break away the adhesions. It was this stage he would remember as he held Julie through the long nights letting her writhe and twist without quite losing her. She suffered from anaemia but also from some obscure virus infection which attacked her legs, sometimes making them swell grotesquely and at other times jack-knifing her with pain. The condition was controllable if she followed her instructions, but she usually did not follow them.

'We're well matched,' he'd say to her, 'a pair of cripples holding one another up.' He said this because that was the year he had to wear a leather corset which supported his spine and (perhaps) was the reason why eventually he recovered so completely that hard physical labour was no bother to him. But he had been blooded. He knew pain to the bone and he thought he would know for the rest of his life how to react to it in others. That was one reason why the girl's rejection of his overtures had worried him. She looked rather worse than better and he wondered if there was anybody she cared for on hand. He remembered that she was the odd one among a large family of Galway horse-breeders who had gone bankrupt and moved to Dublin. He doubted if she would have any more to say now than she had ever had to her elderly parents.

His own life in his mother's flat was far from unpleasant. She seemed to take the greatest care not to crowd him and she left his delightful room alone after she finished painting the door. Sometimes a day went by when he hardly saw her; she was attending weaving classes now three times a week. He found frequent notes from her around the kitchen and that at least brought him back to childhood. On the day he returned with his laundry there was a note propped against the coffee pot, and written as always in her elegant, loosely flowing script: 'If you like, Ben, and only if, go to my room and climb up to the attic. See you for dinner 7.30? Why not concoct one of your pretty desserts if you will be in? I may bring home a friend and you do the same if you like. There's a huge ragout in the slow oven and I'll make a garlicy salad to go with it. Love O.'

He turned over the note written on thick blue paper, and he grinned. It was so typical of her – leaving him free and tugging a string at the same time. And he could do worse, he supposed, if he had anybody to invite. In the week he'd been home he had met some of the old crowd around the pubs and he was meeting another fellow this afternoon in town. The trouble was they were not the old crowd any more. Their names were the same, that was all. When they used to dump their crash helmets under his bed in the hospital and spend hours hanging around Dandelion Green with him on Saturdays and Sundays they were all heads. They wanted to get out of the rat race, as he did, and they talked for hours about going all together to a Greek island to live by mending fishermen's nets or picking peaches, shelling almonds, making hippy jewellery (there was one guy who was going to teach the rest). The plan was to sleep on the beaches in summer and make enough money to rent a little flat-roofed island house in winter where they could smoke their pot and play their Rolling Stones and screw their women until the spring came. Nobody wanted to join a bank or take a Master's Degree or get into the Civil Service. Nobody wanted to teach. Nobody wanted a house in Celbridge and a mortgage and a car and a wife and three kids. They might form a group because there were a couple of good guitarists. They might busk in Paris. They might go back to Delft and find a squat again. They might rent an island in Clew Bay and mend the abandoned cottages to live in. They might stop the bastards killing seal cubs. They might go to California. To Brittany. Where in fact had they all gone?

He had only met six or seven of the heads and they were heads no longer. They were secretaries of insurance companies who took their wives to Rhodes every June. They were account executives in advertising companies, they were in the bank, they were auctioneers, they were producers in RTE. All had a mortgage and most had a wife. One had a lover of his own sex and lived in unbelievable splendour in County Meath. Nobody like himself had a rucksack which could easily carry all he owned and nobody lived with his mother.

Ben turned her note over again and smiled at it. Then he wrote on the back: 'I'll do a vulgar baked Alaska when I get back and I'll leave the ice-cream ready made. Expect *one* for dinner. Love B.'

On his way up to put away his clothes he opened the door of her room. All the windows of this flat faced south and her room too was full of dandelion sunshine. It had yellow-washed walls and white woodwork and many prints in black frames. There were bookshelves under the curving window-seat and more little hanging shelves. She had a recessed wall entirely covered with Ruth Brandt cats (lithographs) and on her divan was a fringed báinín cover with dark gold tweed cushions. Just like at home, another recessed wall held a mahogany chest with a serpentine front and above it her memory wall, framed photographs of himself and Alison, as babies in school uniforms, holding parchments in full academic rig, balanced on motor bikes, lying with their young father on the beach. In the middle of them all was the oval gilt-framed wedding portrait of her and Denis, she trying hard to look like the lady Guinevere (making love to the camera, as they say) and not succeeding too badly, he looking handsome too but obviously wishing it were all over.

Ben stared fixedly at himself on graduation day and noted

with pleasure his open-neck shirt and his bare skinny arms coming out of the gown when everybody else wore a tie. He remembered his other gesture of defiance – white leather clogs which did not feature in the photograph. They clonked satisfactorily all the way up the new parquet floor in the gymnasium while he was making his way to the President's dais. *Non serviam* said the clogs.

'*Non serviam*,' he said now, standing alone in the middle of his mother's room, and then he looked behind a tall black Japanese screen ornamented with flying herons and there behind it was the little staircase which led to the attic.

Up there was a huge sloping skylight which spilled down sun on an abandoned picture in oils (he presumed that weaving had taken over). It was a stiff, feeble still-life of flowers in a blue jar. Very new-looking tubes of paint and some half-empty ones lay about on an old kitchen table which he remembered well. She had used a breadboard as a palette and on it were a few rags stiff with blue paint. There was a copper jug of silvery honesty which presumably had been intended as another subject, and then near the two bentwood chairs under another skylight was the loom, with ropes of wool hanging nearby and something set up. The new artistic future? She would surely be more usefully engaged growing carnations.

Down in the kitchen again, he realised he couldn't make ice-cream because the only cream in the house was solid in the freezer and would need several hours before it became malleable. So because he found a couple of blocks of dark chocolate in the cupboard he made chocolate mousse and turned it into shallow glasses. The cream would be ready to whip by evening and he thought he might bring home some walnuts. Julie used to laugh at his capacity to make pretty-looking desserts which he'd been doing since he was a child. When he forced his memory he thought he had probably started all this when Alison had learned at school to make shortbread. At one stage keeping ahead of her was important to him, because she was a couple of years younger and learning very fast. He thought it fortunate he had lost all sense of competition with her now. A husband, a desirable antique doll's house only a stone's throw from Ballsbridge, two children and a French au pair girl constituted a considerable head-lead. He cleared up in the kitchen, moved the daffodils out of the direct sunlight and headed for town.

He didn't much like the pub where he was to meet Reynolds, but then he didn't much like Reynolds either. They had been in the same class in St Mark's, friends of convenience because they lived not far away from one another. Reynolds had nearly been sacked once for terrorising a junior into handing over his pocket money every Friday. It had gone on for a year before being discovered by a gym master and the only reason Reynolds wasn't sacked was because his uncle was the President and he had argued that, disgraceful though the affair was, Reynolds had never actually *done* anything to the younger boy. This turned out to be a fact. Reynolds had merely threatened to have him beaten up on the way home. It was a long time ago but there was a lot of the old Reynolds left, in the charming smile, the air of total conviction about every opinion he expressed, the pale blue eyes set close together and the low, confidential voice. His clothes were carefully casual and he wore a narrow blue silk tie.

'Good to see you, Ben,' he said, the handgrip warm and tight. 'You're better known in Europe than around these parts recently. What's the line?'

'Nothing at the moment,' Ben said, instantly alert.

'Tough old times,' Reynolds agreed, 'even over in England, I hear, thanks to Mrs T. What can I get you?'

'I'll have a pint.'

'You'd be a long time waiting for the same medicine over in Cologne or wherever you came from?'

'Eindorfen,' Ben said. 'And yes. There are compensations being home again, certainly. What's your own line?'

46

'I'm into importing this while back. Small machinery, computer parts, that sort of thing . . . Partner in the old man's firm since last year.'

'Congratulations. A house in Castleknock and two kids?'

'Something like that. Cheers, Ben.'

'Cheers. Do you ever see any of the old crowd now?'

'Frequently. We have this scheme going to help youngsters leaving the old ranch. The unemployment situation is frightful here this while back.'

'I've heard.'

'So we do what we can for the old firm, if you understand me.'

'I thought the Knights took care of all that sort of thing. Provided the boy is the right colour, so to speak.'

'Ah, Ben, don't you well know all that is greatly exaggerated by people who'd like to get into the Knights if they could? It's always been the same – gross exaggeration by the begrudgers. No, what our little group does is make openings available in any of our lines to fellows from the old shop who need a little leg up when they quit college or wherever. We provide an opening foothold so to speak, and it's available to most young fellows who need it. Once the guy is in somewhere, he's on his own, if you understand me.'

'You mean you don't bail him out of trouble by using the Mafia again?'

'Not at all – get along with you. Mafia!' Reynolds gave his schoolboy titter (again, that hadn't changed much) but his eyes were calculating.

'From time to time in my game we need men with experience of foreign customs and a smattering of the old German, French or Spanish can be useful too.'

'Have another one of those. I confess you have me baffled.'

'No, Ben, let me. I had a run of rare luck at Leopardstown during the week. Care for a chaser?'

'No thanks, a pint is fine.' The order was given and a smooth joke exchanged with the curate. Then Reynolds became businesslike again.

'I take it you have a wee bit of time on your hands at the moment, Ben?'

'I'm not working at the moment, if that's what you mean. You could call this a holiday.'

'Of course, fine. But you could be of assistance to us and make a few notes with very little trouble to yourself. If we can have the right man in the right place at the right time we're prepared to pay him a bit more than necessary.'

'So far the obscurity of your proposition (if that's what it is) is total. What is it you have in mind?'

'Briefly – and I don't want to go into more detail than necessary at this stage – briefly there has been a little trouble lately about computer parts – some of them as minuscule as they are vital – which are made here but *not* unfortunately to the required standard. We import a certain number of them directly for special clients and we don't blow any trumpets about it. We've found the best way is to get them in as personal luggage which saves long hold-ups in vital repairs. We *do* buy Irish whenever we can, mind. But as I said, it isn't always advisable. We've found the person least likely to be searched in detail is the conservatively dressed, vaguely old-fashioned civil service type – good suit, baggy-trousered rather than knife creased and probably with a tweed hat and tie and a strong smell of tobacco rather than after-shave. You get the picture? I must say, Ben, you look somewhat baffled!'

'I'm staggered. You're asking me to take a job as a professionally costumed smuggler, if I understand you.'

'Well, that's being a wee bit hard, isn't it? What I have in mind for you is a little trip once a fortnight or so with an even thousand all clear at the end of every month – it would be the same whether you did one or two trips. You'd be helping us as well as yourself and you'd be helping employment too.'

'Helping employment by smuggling in computer parts

which are made in Ireland?'

'Helping employment by keeping the foreign industrialists happy and ticking over – it's they who will still provide most of the extra jobs we need.'

'How exactly do I come by these pieces of equipment supposing I even considered it? I buy them directly at some agreed suppliers in Düsseldorf or wherever?'

'Not exactly. They have to be selected by somebody who knows what he's doing. I'd give you the contact whom you would phone before collecting the parts from him.'

'All neatly parcelled and sealed in a little package which I shall put in the case for my electric shaver — except that I won't be carrying an electric shaver. People who are required to work a little harder for their thousand a month may have to swallow some little plastic packets and retrieve them at the appropriate end of their persons.' He looked carefully around the flashy, two-thirds empty pub at this hour of the afternoon. 'Something tells me we are talking about hard drugs, Reynolds, are we not? Something tells me we are at least talking about cocaine and we may be talking about heroin!'

'What an extraordinary accusation, Ben! On not even the flimsiest evidence. Bosom friends we may not have been in the old days but by God I thought you knew me better than that. Tell me, do you ever see the Boss Flanagan at all these days?'

The transition from wounded friend to casual gossip was so smooth that it was suspicion itself. Ben found the effrontery of the man almost admirable.

'Never. Is he in the game too?' Reynolds obviously made a quick decision to ignore this.

'Poor Boss had a little manufacturing business booming for him two years ago – he had a flair for it, just like his old man – and the recession has done for him too. The factory folded and the wife died the same month. Those of us still staying afloat have a lot to be grateful for. Now I have to get back to see a client, Ben – why don't you give me a buzz if you reconsider what we've been talking about? One of those numbers will always find me. God bless. It was great seeing you again old son.'

Cheshire smile lingering still, he was gone, leaving Ben shaking his head and biting his lip at the same time. So this was how a godfather looked while he was about his reprehensible business – blue-suited and glossy, chatting innocently of old school friends, doing good by giving a leg-up to the deserving young, charitable and forgiving when he was cruelly misjudged. There was hardly any doubt at all what he was about. It was incredible. Only four or five years ago the likes of Reynolds would have been into car sales or double-glazing. Ben sat for a while longer nursing his pint and watching the bar fill up with lush types as the afternoon became evening. It used to be mainly students here, scruffy, noisy, buying their grass for the weekend, making a couple of pints last until hunger drove them elsewhere, so unused to any more that some of them became truculent if four pints came their way. Now shorts rather than Guinness were the order of the day, though the pub's former clientele (who had moved along when the prices rocketed) were the reason why a good pint was still pulled here for those who wanted it. But looking along the tables he could see few pints. The beautiful people, together after work before they tragically parted for the weekend, favoured tequila or Pernod or gin and tonic or cocktails. They dressed brightly as tropical birds and they sought one another out from table to table, frequently shrieking with delight on discovering somebody, embracing theatrically and loudly exchanging gossip. Very few of these people were in fact theatre people – their watering place was across the road and that was where new productions were frequently cast. But here the common link was business, advertising, travel, sound recording, and the happy sloshers all around him were probably at the top of the heap. He knew very few of them and in fact was astonished to find a hand left companionably on his shoulder.

'Hello Ben. Sorry I missed you when you were over last week. What will you have?'

The smile was very friendly but it took a while to place the face. It was blond and bearded and the eyes were intensely blue. Alison's husband, of course, whose business was architecture.

'Hello Colm, good to see you. As a matter of fact I was thinking of pushing off. The parents are – I mean my mother is entertaining tonight and I'm counted on to turn up.'

'Come over and have one drink with us then – here's Alison.'

They went together, Colm and Alison, like a couple dreamed up by the art directors all around them: both blond as though they belonged to the same family, both about the same height, both fitted to be reliable consumers by virtue of their two salaries, both at home in any crowd such as this and anxious to draw in an outsider if he was the right sort of outsider. The unkindness of his own pigeon-holing suddenly struck Ben forcibly as he was kindly welcomed and plied with the small Jameson he requested. It was early to be getting weary of cosiness, very early indeed to be getting impatient with his native city.

This was Dublin, dreamed of often in the rigours of working abroad. Then it was the very cosiness of Dublin that seemed a virtue, the fact that in no meeting place could you ever be alone, ever encounter a group of people who had never heard of you or of your family and who cared not at all whether you proposed to spend Friday night alone or in company.

'For once,' Alison was saying, 'we are glad poor Monique never wants to go out even on a Friday night. So why don't you come with us and have a meal? Colm has heard of this little place only a few miles from Enniskerry . . .'

'Sorry,' Ben said. 'I'm booked in at home.' He had baulked for a moment at the use of the word and then decided what the hell? Home is where your rucksack is, where you put your clean clothes away, where the book you left open on the floor will still be open when you get back. Home. But it seemed strange applied to the elegant apartment that was all Olivia's rather than his mother's. He sometimes found himself insanely longing for the cobwebby shed at the back of the old house where he was allowed to stable his motor bike. There were hooks all over the ceiling where you could hang up tyres or spare parts and there was an old storm lantern for when it got dark. Sometimes there would be as many as eight or nine fellows all packed into the smoky room discussing problems, offering theories about the current gearbox trouble, suggesting where such and such a part might be found cheap, doing deals with one another for machines they owned – very often they owned more than one machine and very often they still had no transport, or 'wheels', as they said to one another, because no machine was in working order. Having wheels was very important, summer or winter. Having wheels was status and a way of life. It could mean the difference between taking a woman (all girls were women then) to a mountain lake on a summer's afternoon or to the local park. It could mean roaring off into a summer's night with your sleeping bag strapped to the back, heading down with the gang for a weekend in somebody's parents' cottage in Wexford maybe. Having wheels was the antidote to school and stability. It meant change at a whim and independence.

Where were they now, all the bikers? Sitting with their wives or long-term girl friends in a pub like this, Japanese cars outside waiting to take them home or maybe to the sort of little place near Enniskerry that Alison had in mind?

'Olivia has been talking about you ever since that day you came over,' Alison was saying. 'She's asked to be let stay up if you're coming to dinner one evening. I told you I'm trying to arrange a family get-together, didn't I, Colm?'

'Good idea,' said Colm and he actually seemed to mean it.

'You mean Mother and Dad?' Ben asked.

'Yes, well, they must meet some time. It's only civilised, but there just doesn't seem to have been the excuse. You're that excuse now.'

'I'm not sure you know what you're taking on,' Ben said gently.

'Look, I've been thinking about it and I won't invite anybody until I'm sure. Meanwhile you should drop over yourself whenever you like. But phone first to make sure I'm there.'

'Of course,' Ben said, and refused Colm's offer to drop him somewhere. He had wanted to tell them about Reynolds and his amazing proposition but it was difficult to find the words. Somebody like Reynolds would be even more incomprehensible to them than to himself. Ben obscurely felt that trying to understand his own instability at the age of twenty-seven was probably as far as Alison and Colm could be expected to go. It was perhaps an unkind mistake to regard them as smug. They were quite concerned in their own way so long as they did not feel threatened. They left him cheerfully and even affectionately in South Anne Street. He bought walnuts for the dessert in a late-closing delicatessen before going to catch his bus in Nassau Street.

5

Only a few blocks away, although Ben couldn't know it, his mother was sitting over a drink with the headmaster of an inner city school. They had chosen this wine bar carefully because it was unlikely that either of them would know anybody here. It was a place which had been deliberately designed to evoke the thirties, bentwood chairs with cane seats, low-hanging cane lampshades over every table sending a spill of light onto the posies of fresh flowers. The walls were covered with old family photographs, sepia prints of haymaking long ago, country weddings, little girls with dresses tucked into their knickers making sandcastles, side-cars full of people in straw hats setting off with hampers. Neither Olivia nor Stephen could possibly imagine that anybody they knew would come here, so they lingered over the chilled French white wine which the place specialised in. From the odd word exchanged at exhibitions or in the homes of mutual friends they had progressed to the occasional meeting of this sort. Stephen did most of the talking while Olivia sat listening with total attention. This evening he was longer than usual talking out what was bothering him.

'This latest calamity is typical,' he was saying. 'There was no reason to suppose Matt O'Leary wasn't satisfied – as satisfied as you can be in a school where most of the kids have no hope of bettering themselves anyway, and very few want to. But Matt wasn't only a first-class maths teacher. He had the common touch and it sounds pretentious but there's no other way to describe it. He's a scholarship boy himself, son of a widowed country schoolmistress from a Cork village at the back of beyond, and once my fellows got over jeering at his accent and trying to topple him (they found they couldn't), he got through to them as nobody else ever did before. He was even capable of besting the few thugs who waited to beat him up after school in the early days. Without doing him any more serious harm, he bloodied the nose of one of them and tied another fellow up in such a knot with arms pinned behind his back that the fellow climbed down pretty fast from his plan to do for the new culchie master. Matt is a big guy, big soft good-humoured face under the red hair and it was natural for my lot to regard him as easy game. But after he had changed their minds for them, he never looked back. He has a fine mathematical brain and the patience of Job in class – that is where the work is involved. Otherwise his method is a savage blast of anger at the first sign of messing and that's usually the end of it. You see the thing is, he likes the kids, always has, and feels for their hopeless lives in a way that somehow gets through to them. He's willing to spend endless time after class with them, too, and he got a football club going in no time.'

'Now he wants out?' Olivia said, playing with her glass. It was unusual for her to glance at her watch while in Stephen's company but she did now.

'I'm holding you up?'

'No, no. But I have to make a phone call. Excuse me.'

When she came back he had ordered more wine, and was smiling hopefully at her. 'I don't suppose you could have a meal with me this evening? We don't have to stay here unless you particularly like their delicious healthful salad and quiche over there. Why don't we have a starter here and then go somewhere else?'

'Sorry,' Olivia said. 'My son Ben is eventually expecting me

55

to turn up for a meal. I've just told him I'll be a little late. Why don't you join us?'

It was so casually put that there was no difficulty. She knew about his wife anyway, and he knew about Denis.

'I'd love to do that.'

'Wonderful. Now go on about Matt O'Leary. Why can't you offer him more money?'

'In the first place, he wouldn't be interested even if I could. He doesn't seem to be ambitious in that way at all. And in the second place he's already handed in his notice. He'll work until the end of the term and that's it. It's very unusual for a schoolmaster not to work out the academic year, so I know he must be at the end of his tether. Says he wants to take a year out in the United States – some bursary or other. But I know it isn't just that.'

'What is it?'

The schoolmaster sighed. 'It's the futility of educating them for the streets – that's it I think. Some of them are involved in crime and drugs already. Many of them come from petty criminal homes. A few have brothers or fathers who are major criminals and serving life sentences. It's the fact that you can't win. They're doomed anyhow. The Government doesn't give a shit about them because it's supported by the mass of the middle classes and there are no votes in education anyhow. Some remedial teaching has actually been cut back, and I've recently had to increase the size of classes. You're talking about a sort of human scrap-heap. But I've bothered you enough about my problems. How about yours?'

'None really. I've converted the attic although I know I'm fooling myself trying to paint. I'm taking lessons in weaving now as well.'

'I've always hoped you might show me something some-time. Maybe you will tonight. How can I agree or disagree with your unkind verdict otherwise? You may not be wasting your time although I can only offer an uninformed opinion.'

'Thank you but no thanks.' Olivia smiled.

'My wife', he said carefully, 'used to be quite good and that's a sort of coincidence – with your painting I mean – that gives me some hope.'

'I don't think I quite understand that.'

'I'm sorry,' he said quickly. 'Forget it. Do you have the car in town?'

'No I walked in, because it was so fine.'

'Then we can drive out there together and you can show me the way.'

When they arrived Ben was shelling walnuts in the kitchen and the table was laid for three. The introduction was casually made before Olivia threw off her jacket and set about shredding vegetables for the salads. They settled the visitor with a glass of wine in front of the fire in the other room.

'How did your day go, love?' she said to Ben exactly as he remembered her saying to his father.

'Very like a whale. Had the offer of a job as a matter of fact.'

'You don't mean it? In this city at this time after only a week. You're joking?'

He laughed at her delighted face as he spread a layer of chopped walnuts on his confection.

'Don't open the champagne yet until I tell you, Mother.'

She remembered Reynolds, of course. She was the only person he knew who called him Fintan. When he gave her the details she looked thoughtful.

'Of course you may be jumping to wild conclusions about Fintan but even if you are not, I'd hardly recommend smuggling as a career. At any rate you're on holiday aren't you? There's no need to bother about anything yet.' Her comparatively calm reaction amazed him and he changed the subject.

'Your attic conversion job is most efficient,' he said. 'I wouldn't be qualified to give a snap judgement on your painting but I'm glad you've started again.'

'It was only a beginning,' she said quickly, 'a way of

57

structuring the day. I'm taking weaving lessons now.'

When he looked down at her face he saw she was indeed, as he suspected, thinking of his father again and the broken routines of thirty years.

'Can I talk to you about it sometime?' he said.

'If you like. Any time.'

'But not now.'

'No, not now.' She smiled quickly and set the promised garlicy salad in the middle of the table in a large wooden bowl. It looked pretty as a flower garden and he said so. Then he went to fetch the guest while she took the casserole out of the oven and set a basket of potatoes baked in their jackets beside the salad.

Nothing, Ben decided, could have been easier than that meal with his mother and the man who (for all he knew) might be her lover. They looked about the same age, and the man knew enough about her to have brought along her favourite wine. His manner too was very confident. Yet if he was her lover what was the meaning of that sentence about structuring her day? Structuring took care of itself if you had somebody to act as a reference point. Strangely he didn't find it difficult to imagine her as somebody's woman. What she still had was a way of making people feel important by her interest in them, a way of dressing that was different from her contemporaries and casually youthful, and she had never put on weight. In a soft light like tonight's you would have to feel her skin to be sure she was not young. The schoolmaster seemed delighted with her, but now Ben was being addressed and he had better pay attention.

'What did you do before you cut loose, Ben?'

'I was a maths teacher,' Ben said and couldn't understand the man's instant reaction and the broad white smile that settled and stayed on his face. His mother got up and went to the oven.

'Do you mind my asking where you taught?'

'Sandymount High School.'

'So boys and girls together in class present no problem to you?'

'Not at the moment since I don't teach any more.' This was becoming a bore.

'If you reconsidered that – if we could even talk about it – I'd be for ever grateful to you. The fact is –' Ben listened to the very brief statement of the man's problem and he was still laughing when his mother returned to the table. She was smiling.

'Two offers of a job in one day! It's something I never thought I'd have to worry about in Dublin,' Ben said genuinely baffled. 'Is it a plot?'

'Not of mine,' said Olivia quickly. 'I knew Stephen needed a maths teacher but I naturally wouldn't mention you – without consulting you first.'

'Will you come to see me next week, Ben,' the headmaster wanted to know, 'even if it's only to look over our school?'

'OK. I'd even be interested to look over your school in view of where it is.'

'A maths teacher who specialises in chocolate mousse,' the man said thoughtfully spooning it up. 'You may be what I've been waiting for all my life.'

'Don't be too sure you've found me,' Ben said sourly enough. Again he was overcome by the cosiness of all this, the apparent conspiracy of the fates to land him back where he started. Was it for this he had done the exile bit, learned a little about the world and a fair amount about himself? Yet in this city where there was apparently an interesting job waiting for him Julie had come home to roost too. And it wasn't the pleasant city he had left. It was now a ravaged, hopeless, violent city, and it wasn't promising him a rose garden. It was at least worth thinking about. So he said later to his mother when the man had gone home, leaving Ben vaguely wondering if he might have stayed the night had they been alone together.

59

'I wouldn't want you to feel any of this had been plotted,' she said anxiously to him. 'I only heard it myself this afternoon – about the wonderful maths teacher Matt O'Leary, I mean, and his determination to go. What's particularly worrying to Stephen is that he won't stay until the summer, which of course is the usual thing.'

'Of course. Well I'm going to think about it – even if I only stay to help him out for the summer term. I don't want to talk about that now though, I want to talk about you and Dad – if you don't mind, I mean.'

She was sitting where she had always sat, when only her family was present, cross-legged on the hearthrug with her hands open in the hollow of her skirt. She looked up quickly at him in the dying glow of the fire.

'What is there to talk about?' she said at last. 'We married, we stayed together until you were all reared, and now we're pursuing at last our own lives which we might have done long ago if you hadn't had to be considered. It's a fairly ordinary story, after all.'

'But you seemed to belong together. You didn't fight or have scenes.'

'We're not the fighting sort. Our battles were largely silent. But what I felt in the end was that I had to find out if there was anything I could contribute for *myself* to the whole business of being alive on this planet for a strictly limited few years.'

'You mean your painting?'

'Not necessarily. I mean pursuing my life as a free individual. Helping where I can, saying "I" where I have always said "We". Thinking as I. I don't suppose it's easy for you to understand.'

'It's very easy for me to understand. But what about him? Would it be vulgar to ask you if he was unfaithful and if that precipitated the break?'

'It would, but I don't mind telling you. He wasn't and if he was it was only with his work which will soon be over now. I can't be certain, but I think he wasn't unfaithful.'

'Were you?' They had always had extraordinary conversations, all four of them, in view of their relationship, but Ben knew he wouldn't have asked this so boldly in the old days.

'Very briefly, yes. But I thought it would be nice to be entirely free to do as I wished at the end of my life.' The response to this was obvious but he made it.

'It's not the end of your life.'

'It's the last one-third for sure. And I like being free, to strike up conversations, fraternise with a variety of people, travel where I please without consulting anybody. I suppose in a way it's getting back to the freedom of youth only better. Less restricted because one *knows*. I don't deny that this whole outlook is selfish in the extreme – in fact I say positively that it is. And I don't deny there could come a time when I would want to live with Denis again from free choice.'

'You think that could be so easily arranged?'

'Not at *all*. If the time ever came the whole thing would be next door to impossible unless he were feeling exactly the same way.'

'He didn't want this separation as you did?'

'He never wants change of any kind. Change is challenge, but he didn't hesitate. He gave me without hesitation my freedom and my share of everything we had built up together. He is, you see, too honourable for his own good. I didn't even have to be told that by his friends, although of course I was.'

'Did it ever occur to you that he too might be enjoying his freedom?'

'Not particularly, because he was always free. Men always are.'

'Not, surely, honourable men who have made commitments for life?'

'I don't think you ever cease feeling free as we do. It's almost always the man who walks out of a marriage, not the woman. If he does he knows that the children will still be cared for and their physical environment will be much the same. So that gives him the advantage.'

'All this is more than a bit muddled,' Ben said. 'I find it hard to believe you considered all these sociological facts before you made your decision to walk out on him after a lifetime in his company.'

'I can't help that,' she smiled. 'It's your difficulty, not mine.'

He was dissatisfied with the whole thing. He had a vague sense of grievance which made him want to hurt her as when he deliberately chose the gift of the little carpet.

'Were you,' he said at last, when she turned away to stare into what was left of the fire, 'were you in love with him when you married?'

'Yes and no,' she said helpfully. 'There was somebody else with whom I had had a hopeless, passionate affair a few years previously. Denis was calm and devoted and I think we probably invented the love bit, both of us. We believed we were in love, that's all I can say.'

Again it strengthened his sense of grievance, that calm analysis of hers. Cold-blooded and less than frank was his eventual verdict. And as often before, she took the wind out of his sails.

'Let's invite him over here one evening, Ben,' she said, turning the conscious charm so forcibly on him that he felt obliged to resist it.

'Don't you think that might be a bit corny? Like something Alison would do?'

'Alison will do it, almost certainly. She's mentioned it. But that wouldn't be at all the same. You and I could entertain him here as we did Stephen tonight. I can't believe he would refuse and it would be lovely to have that sort of evening again, just the three of us.'

'Yes,' said Ben, bored. 'But are you sure he would accept the invitation? If you're not it would be better not to invite him.'

'I don't think he'd refuse.'

'Let's see how it goes before we do anything,' said Ben vaguely. He was out of harmony with her and had no intention of playing along. Looking around at the comfort she had created, he was grateful to her but he resented it at the same time. He began to remember the impatience with home that had driven him away the first time.

6

St Domenic's was not the sort of school you could run on conventional lines and Stephen Lydon made no attempt to do it. So far as possible there was no rollcall. Teachers were instructed to make note of absences some time around mid-morning. There might be any number of reasons why a pupil could be late, most of them related to the chaotic conditions of life at home. Most of the children preferred school to home anyway and if they finally achieved their arrival, however late, there was good reason for not victimising them or even making them feel embarrassed. For the same reason pupils who needed help to buy textbooks simply came privately to him in his office and stated their reasons. He preferred to take a chance on the fact that they might be lying. Most of them told the truth, stark and simple. Free secondary education had to be just that before they could avail themselves of it. Their parents' contribution was not in the form of large voluntary contributions at the beginning of every term, as in middle-class areas. Their parents' contribution was the loss of their earnings. Not that this was as relevant a reason as it used to be. There were few conventional jobs going now – no jobs for messenger boys, few for apprentices and virtually none for casual dockers. Container goods had killed the docks and there were weeds growing around and over the warehouses where the St Domenic's parents used to work. The docks were dead and with them job prospects for the thousands of ill-educated youths. The best that school could do for them was to make them literate, able to handle the small income they would grow into from the social welfare schemes, able to sign the dole and apply for the jobs that were no longer there, able to read the racing form for use in the few remaining bookies' offices, able to read the newspapers and the street notices. Many of the boys in particular left St Domenic's at fifteen or sixteen able to do no more. They were the lucky ones. The unfortunates dropped out after four or five years of futile attempts at literacy, and their lives from that point onward could only be a down graph. A day seldom passed that Stephen didn't see one of his former pupils mentioned in the daily papers – among reports from the criminal courts. Sometimes the name astonished him, but more often he had silently and resignedly foretold to himself a particular boy's future.

Matt O'Leary was the first teacher he had ever employed who was prepared to spend part of his free time with the pupils, boys in particular. Generally speaking, girls made better use of their time here and only the predictables left school as far from literacy as when they arrived. These came from illiterate homes where there was a drink or drugs problem or both. You could pick out the dead little faces, but children subject to sexual abuse at home (a growing problem) were harder to spot. Violence of one sort or another was endemic in this area and it usually happened when weekend drinking got out of control. Organised crime was a recent but increasing pressure on these children's lives. Stephen thought less of sociological problems than of faces with names to them. The day Ben called, for instance, was one of the worst days he could remember, because soon after break that morning Brian Collopy had been carried into his office unconscious from an overdose of smack self-administered in the lavatory. The headmaster asked Ben to wait in an ante-room while an ambulance and the police were called. Through the glass partition Ben could see the thin ten-year-old carried out on a stretcher, giggled at nervously by fellow pupils clustered together in the hall. Later he was told the boy was sixteen, not ten years old.

'It's as well for you to learn the worst any day can bring if you do consider working for us, Ben,' the headmaster said, when at last there was time for an interview. 'Brian Collopy was the bright one of that family and he played a sweet tin whistle until some time last year. The wonder is that he's still at school despite the state he's in. He survived his Inter Cert. and was full of spunk before his mother died. The fellow who gave him his first shot of heroin was most likely his brother who came over for the funeral – a junkie from Brixton with a criminal record. He pushed the stuff on a small scale to feed his habit. He was an unimportant cog in a big wheel. The police seldom get the big fellows. He's in jail now again.'

'What will happen to Brian?'

The headmaster shrugged. 'Immediately, detoxification in Jervis Street. Then what should happen in six months or more is a rehabilitation centre like Coolmine but it won't happen because there aren't enough places. He'll come back home to the exact conditions that made him what he is and he may return to school because he's a fighter. But it will happen again. Most of his friends are junkies and small-time criminals, several of them in this school. It's a vicious circle that needs a really serious crash programme to break it, but the Government is not prepared to pay for that. You learn to live with the Brians of this school and even to understand them. Smack is their way of escape from the intolerable. They don't know until it's too late that the escape route leads to a black hole. Excuse me,' he ended abruptly. The headmaster left Ben in the rather stark office whose only aspiration to gracious living was the absence of graffiti on the walls. All the way up the stairs and in the hall he had marvelled at the way the rest of the open spaces were plastered with them – HENNO IS SHIT FRANK THE WANK KISS MY ASS HAZEL PULLS ME OFF IN THE

HIVE CANT DO IT COLLOPY CUNT-FACE COME
HOME FRANKIE SAYS RELAX – this last had the accom-
panying sketch of a smiling twig-legged boy whose flies revealed an extensive erection. There was another quite com-
petent sketch labelled HAZEL COMBS HER HARE. Hazel's
pubic hair reached to the ground. Some were written with a
red spray can, most with thick markers or chalk, and almost all
of them mis-spelled.

Ben walked from the headmaster's desk to the tall uncur-
tained window and looked down at the desolation of the city
below. The cleared sites which used to be tenement houses full
of neighbourly life were car parks now, covered over with
gravel. A handful of Georgian terraces still stood in this north
side of the city, one or two restored and lived in on the edge of
the abyss, most with collapsed walls and partly demolished
roofs (the lead having been stripped away by vandals). A house
directly opposite the window where he stood had the wall
nearest to the school fallen out in a heap of rubble onto the
pavement, so that passers-by had to walk on the road.
Through the gaping wound you could see all the chimney-
pieces on that side of the house, the colours people had chosen
for their surroundings, the remains of wallpaper. One room at
the top had its floor mysteriously intact and on it stood a
rickety table with a kettle on it. A picture hung crookedly on
the wall above it and there was a tin on a shelf. A small square
window frame had partly collapsed but a length of sooty net
curtain still clung to it, all that remained of a family home.
These people, whoever they were, had quite possibly been
moved to a failed municipal housing experiment further north
in Ballymun where towers twenty and more storeys high were
gradually crumbling away from inadequate heating and van-
dalism. Families there were clamorous to be moved back to
this inner city again. Ben remembered going to Ballymun once
with his father in search of a jobbing gardener and seeing the
rubbish piled up at every corner and the total absence, at that

period, of pavements. The towers rose grey out of the rubbish dumps into a grey sky. There was neither a tree nor a flower to be seen although the scheme at that stage was ten years old. A thin whine of children's voices came from the balconies from which a baby had fallen to its death some time around then. Now, twenty years afterwards, organised crime flourished there among the grown-up babies and the drug problem was crucial. He tried to imagine himself working there or in this school as the headmaster returned to glance briefly at the CV which Ben had put on his desk.

'Well, Ben, as you see, I can't offer you a rose garden. But if you'll help us out just for the summer term you'll be doing one of the corporal works of mercy. I see you have experience of tough manual labour. I can certainly offer you a bit of that. We're trying to build a swimming pool with inadequate help from the Department.'

Ben was glad he wasn't at this stage being treated as his mother's son. The financial arrangements discussed were surprisingly good. His hours of duty were long because of short-staffing. He took the job, lured by its difficulty and by the dereliction on every side of him. A rose garden was not what he had come home to find. He was to begin the next day.

It's true that his heart misgave him as he ran downstairs amid the clamour of the midday break. Unflattering comments about his appearance came from every side as he made his way out through the hall; this final exit was followed by an ironic cheer from an overgrown first year with red hair and a pair of punishing Doc Martin boots, popularly known as 'granny bashers'.

That same boy was the first to cause trouble in class the next day.

'Sir,' he leered, 'I can't read your writin', right?'

'Then come up to the front, Luke.' Ben had taken seriously the advice of an older teacher in his first school: 'Try to memorise the buggers' names before you go much further the

68

first day.' He had memorised enough to impress them in the first fifteen minutes.

'The mammy says I'm delicate, sir, and I do have to keep out of the draughts, right?'

'We'll shut this window for you. Come up to the front Luke.'

'I can't, sir, me legs is locked. Like me aul fella last night.'

This sally was greeted with guffaws of approval from the mates and Luke leered around again. Ben tried another tack.

'Would you change places with Luke please Hazel?'

The dark girl in front got promptly to her feet and Luke appeared to be temporarily thrown when she stood before his desk. He let her have his desk, shambled slightly disgruntedly up to hers, big boots scraping along the lino.

'Can you see comfortably now Luke?' Ben asked.

'Go and shag yourself sir,' said Luke as though he were giving a greeting and there was a slight intake of breath from the class which Ben decided to ignore.

'Well, as we were saying before Luke experienced his difficulty, the values change if you look at the problem like this. Turn to page twenty-four and see how the thing is set out there. Then watch what happens when I change the tack.'

They were slow to follow but easy to interest in any little short-cut. The removal of Luke from the back now improved things considerably down there. Ann O'Connell appeared to be interested in her work and the few questions she asked were relevant. He set a problem to solve for themselves and then he seated himself on the edge of his desk with a textbook and watched them under the guise of reading it.

There were fifty-three of them in front of him and most of them looked extremely clean. What he found touching was the care devoted to their appearance – few of these pupils could have left home without preparing for a final look in some mirror which would satisfy them. A girl in the second row had short bristly green hair, deliberately fixed to stand punk-style on end. Her face underneath was fragile and pale and even studious. Another to the left of her had arranged her black hair African-style in a hundred little pigtails, all with their separate partings on her scalp. A boy at the end of the second row had the blond look of a twenties lawn tennis star, short back and sides but lightly waved and combed back on top. He was fair skinned and blue eyed and his teeth were good. Most of the faces were pale as though they were seldom exposed to the fresh air and two or three of them looked actually ill. Those children hardly appeared to be present in the class at all. They had effaced themselves so effectively that you felt you would have to shout into their ears to reach them.

As he knew would happen (it was only a question of when) a few pupils towards the back started to titter and pass a note around. Some of those who touched it passed it on unlooked at and these Ben suspected of being illiterate rather than conscientious students. He had a theory about incipient trouble which had worked in his last school. Ignore it as long as possible and don't go looking for a big scene. If it happens don't run away from it. So he immersed himself in his textbook and was gradually aware of a subsidence. Then the hands went up one by one.

'Finished sir, me sir, sir.'

The ones who knew what the whole problem was about were anxious to show off just as in any other school. The rest kept their heads down for the time being at any rate. He selected the girl with green hair to demonstrate on the board what she had done, and it was then that the note which had been circulating reached the twenties tennis star at the end of the second row. He suddenly exploded into maniacal laughter and there was no choice. Ben pounced and picked up the note. The writing was not copperplate and the spelling could be improved but the message was clear: *Sirs bollix is maid of sponge cake.* Ben rolled the paper in his hand and dropped it into the waste basket without comment.

'Could you make your figures a little larger, Hazel?' he asked the girl at the blackboard.

'Her tits has the same complaint, sir' came from the second-last row and this time (because the girl was involved) he asked the speaker to stand out at the back of the class and was unexpectedly obeyed. The class wore on without major incident after that and when the bell rang he wrote up their homework on the blackboard and left the classroom. There was a slight persistent pain at the back of his eyelids and he looked forward to coffee.

In the staff-room he was introduced to O'Leary who was staying on to work out the end of this week. The handgrip was tight and friendly and Ben liked the big red-haired man from the first glance.

'Never mind what they'll be saying to you Ben,' O'Leary advised. Those kids are OK. I'll miss the little bastards when I'm out of here but I can't take any more.'

'Why?' Ben asked, filling out vile watery coffee from the machine. He walked with O'Leary to the window which overlooked a block of new Corporation flats.

'Out there is hell,' he said. 'Just remember that. Three weeks ago I knew I'd have to get out or go mad: just remember it's not the fault of those kids. None of it is their fault whatever they may do. Or say.'

'What happened three weeks ago?'

'My mouth is too big, Ben. Forget it.'

On the night before he left, however, Ben had a pint in town with the big man and heard the incredible story of fourteen-year-old Pauline Devlin. From her description Ben formed a picture very like the small girl with green hair in his own class. Pauline had an interest in the football club and had asked Matt to join. One afternoon while they were practising a tall thug had whistled to her and she had rushed away terrified at the first sound without a word of excuse or explanation. The tall thug had turned out to be her brother, the eldest of five

71

brothers. Her mother had died last year and her father was an alcoholic who bred alsatians as watchdogs. Pauline cooked and cleaned for the five brothers and her father and she was frequently late for school. Sometimes she fell asleep in class but always she would be eager to play football afterwards if O'Leary called a practice. One day she collapsed during the game and he carried her unconscious into the staff-room while somebody phoned for a doctor. During the examination it was discovered that the girl was covered in sores from the waist down all with their origin in the genitalia. She was suffering from an acute form of venereal disease and needed immediate hospitalisation. Her story emerged while she was in hospital. At this point the cheerful face of O'Leary seemed to collapse inwards and to Ben's astonishment (even although the sadness of the story got to him too) the big man was weeping into his pint and shaking.

'I'm only telling you because you have to know the hellholes some of them come from, Ben,' he said. 'All five of the filthy bastards and her aul fella were having it off with her regularly since the mother died. They had Pauline too terrorised by the alsatian dogs to get help. She's not even fifteen.'

'Where is she?' Ben felt sick himself now.

'The nuns have her in care for the time being. Foster parents will be found for her and there's a court case pending. If she has to give evidence in public it will be the finish of her. I've already made a sworn statement to the guards and if necessary I'll fly back from the States if they need me in court. But Jesus she shouldn't have to rehash all that again in court. Sworn affidavits should be enough to land the whole hellspawn of them in jail for the rest of their lives.'

'Thanks for telling me,' Ben said quietly, 'but I think they are victims too.'

' 'Tis as well for you to know what you're taking on.'

'Yes.' They stood forlornly together looking into their half-gone pints.

'What in the name of the sweet-suffering Jesus am I doing here?' Ben said then. 'I was out of it, living the not unpleasant life of a rover where I had no commitments except to myself. Here I am back now committed to my agreeable problem family in my own horrendous city full of Pauline Devlins and I haven't a notion of why I'm here. Can you tell me?'

Over the second pint O'Leary tried to get things straight. 'It's hardly a city full of Pauline Devlins. It's a violent, hopeless city that's had the heart torn out of it and it has more Pauline Devlins than are ever reported in the newspapers. More suicides too. You're back, man, because it's your own place. When I left Kerry I thought I was leaving Paradise and when I leave here I'll be leching after the old haunts here in Dublin instead of enjoying the fleshpots while I can. That I know.'

'Where exactly are the fleshpots?'

'Princeton. I got this athletics scholarship that I put in for in some despairing moment, never dreaming I'd get it. Pauline was the last straw. I wrote off accepting it.'

'Why didn't you work out the year?'

'I knew if I did I'd talk myself out of going. Holidays give you a false perspective for the rest of the year. I knew I'd persuade myself I was achieving something in St Domenic's and, for God's sake, that they needed me.'

'They do. I'm a poor substitute for you.'

'Maybe,' O'Leary grinned, 'but you're all they've got now. And I know I was thinking straight when I made up my mind that I've given all I can without driving myself around the bend and then being useless anyway.'

'How long have you been teaching in Domenic's?'

'Going on four years now. It was my first job after I took the H. Dip. At first I thought I wouldn't stick it for a single term.'

'Is it worse or better now?'

'You mean the kids' situation? Worse I'd say. There's a lot more unemployment and the parents take it out on them.

There's a lot more of the drug problem too. After all, their lives *are* hopeless. What have we to offer them?'

'Literacy I suppose. Not much more unless it's a few hours freedom from their homes.'

'I can see you may survive if you have no elevated expectations of what you can do. When I first came up fresh from the country, I was such a gom I thought I could change the whole system. I joined the Labour Party and worked hard for it until I realised that they were as conservative as either of the other camps when there was a hope of office. They aim for power to change the social system but in order to get it they are satisfied to sell themselves down the river. So, in office, they are futile, hamstrung. I don't even vote now. I want out, even if exile crucifies me, which it probably will.'

'You'll come back with even more to offer in the way of athletic training.'

'You've got it wrong, boy. I'll never come back. There's a girl from home over there nursing. I'll marry her if she'll still have me and I'll not rear a family here on the backs of the poor. No bloody fear. But listen to me now and I'll try to save you from some of the worst mistakes I made.'

It was late before they took leave of one another. Ben stood in Nassau Street against the railings to watch with some affection the huge Kerry man getting lost in the nighttime crowds, his flaming head of hair picking him out for a long time under the street lamps. As he waited for his bus to Monkstown Ben felt cold in the warm April evening. All around him were strolling girls in the first of the summer dresses.

7

Denis liked the first soft evenings of April, the sort of evenings when he used to enjoy strolling about his large garden and brooding about odd corners that could be improved. A hydrangea maybe if he could open up that area around the white wall to the light? Feed it copper and tea-leaves and make it blue? A miniature willow beside the so-called dolls' pool? Alison had washed her dolls' clothes there on summer evenings and once killed a couple of goldfish with detergent. He could still see her holding them, slippery in her small hands, asking him why they had died. He had said from old age and had led her gently to the bottom of the garden for their burial. She had wrapped them in tissue paper before she would agree to bury them and he told her the roses would grow better after this extra food. The willow he had planted beside the pool flourished. It was the first thing people admired when they looked out of the kitchen window.

These April days he had no garden to wander around, merely a car park with a small shrubbery behind it and plants standing in tubs at the four corners, but he liked to walk around the familiar avenues and look into other people's gardens. Many of them that he remembered were gone now, their handcut stone walls bulldozed away. Their crocuses and their snowdrops and their daffodils that had multiplied over the years were obliterated now under a bed of concrete for cars to sleep on. One garden in particular used to astonish him all over again every springtime. It was the last one of a Victorian terrace and it was enormous, almost a parkland of beech trees with daffodils sown thickly as grass all over it. You forgot about those daffodils when they died away in long untidy greenery, each April. You forgot them in May and you forgot them in June when they looked like dry brown grasses which eventually would be mowed with the rest – he remembered one old-fashioned jobbing gardener called Pat Birtwhistle using a scythe on them. That garden was like any other (except bigger) for most of the year and then one day in early March you might be walking by and you'd see those hundreds of stiff green spears, sharply pointed, and you would watch them growing paler as the month advanced before suddenly exploding into gold some sunny afternoon around St Patrick's Day. After that, for three or four weeks, people would stand in the avenue outside to look over the wall and catch their breath at the sight of those hundreds of daffodils, their brazen colour making you imagine a haze of gold standing in the air over that house. Those days the old lady called Miss Sandes who lived alone there, the last of all her family, would often be seen on the steps, wrapped in her dead brother's caped ulster, picking dead leaves from the flower pots which she always left out to weather out the winter as best they could. There were large old terracotta flower pots, mossy with the damp, and in spring she would poke in new earth around the tops, sprinkling it here and there with potting compost which she would water in while pausing now and again to look down at her glory of daffodils. When they had faded, those flower pots came to life and all summer long the geraniums blazed away on the steps, needing no more than a sprinkling of water on hot evenings and removal of dead heads which was a job she seemed to like. Denis had known her all his married life but had hardly spoken to her because she never went out and her garden was too long to carry the sound of voices up the steps. But he always called out the time of day to her if she looked up and she would wave

76

her trowel at him. Two ginger cats were usually blinking in the sun beside her. Somewhere indoors was an old servant who did the shopping and cooked for her. It was said by the neighbours that old Mollie had served in that family since they had got her from the orphanage as a girl of fifteen around the time of World War One.

It was a while since Denis had strolled around the corner where Miss Sandes' garden used to be, but he did this evening and remembered her and her cats as he looked over the ruined wall at what progress had done to the place where her house had been. The entire site now held fifty different units of single-bedroomed flats, all encased in brick, each possessing a balcony looking down on the thirty cars which stood where the daffodils used to be. The black wrought-iron gates had been removed to make a wider entrance and the cut-stone wall had been pebble-dashed. In one of those fifty units Anita lived, who at least knew about Miss Sandes and the daffodils because he had told her.

This was not Friday, however, and who knew where Anita might be? At one of her classes no doubt. He strolled along, noting the gardens (five or six) that had not changed much in thirty years, although the trees were bigger. Some of these gardens were even better than they used to be, with pruned well-fed roses smug-looking in their loamy dark soil, their first leaves already springing from the outward-turning buds. These gardens had daffodils too and tightly closed tulips among the rosebeds but the careless glory of the Sandes garden would never be found again in his time.

This district belonged especially to Denis because he had been born here, the son of a chandler whose bright red, gold and black shop had stood at the junction of Rathmines and Rathgar roads. His father had prospered by the time Denis was born and they no longer lived above the shop but in a handsome red-brick house nearer to Dartry. He remembered lying in bed on long summer evenings (his bedtime never varied with the seasons), and listening to the sounds that came up to him from the cobblestoned road outside, the No. 14 tram clanging and rattling on its way to Dartry, the howl of a lonely dog, the dusty sighing of the trees after the long hot day. No cars to go roaring through the night like now, no drunken revellers (not in that district at that time), no transistor radios, nothing but the trees and the awaited whistling of Lady Hogan when the last tram had gone by. There was something magic about Lady Hogan, who was a gentleman. You could hear his beautiful whistling from quite a distance away. You could hear it getting nearer and nearer, and sometimes it stopped. You could jump out of bed and see why it stopped. You could see Lady Hogan dancing around under each street lamp which glowed golden as a daffodil in the long summer twilight. He was small and strange and this was his time because sometimes the big boys jeered at him and annoyed him in the daytime. Evenings were Lady Hogan's. He wore black knee-length breeches and ladies' high buttoned boots. He wore a cap and a Norfolk jacket and he lived alone in a little hut by the river Dodder. Once only at that time had Denis seen him in daylight, and then he realised why the big boys were jeering at him and threatening to throw him into the river. When you looked into Lady Hogan's face you were not sure whether you were looking at a lady or a gentleman. He was puffy and strange around the waistcoat too and his voice was high, not like a man's. But he could get angry and he could curse like a trooper. That day along by the Dodder the big boys were trying to hurtle Lady Hogan in and he was strenuously resisting, shouting reciprocal insults at them in his treble voice. They had first tried to tear off his clothes, guffawing over what they would find underneath. But Lady Hogan had struggled so savagely that they had given this up and were now attempting to throw him fully clothed into his own river. Denis shouted, 'Leave him alone and fight your match!' But in fact Lady Hogan was their match. Slippery as an eel and still cursing he managed to escape and went charging in his high button boots up the steep hill to the Dartry Road where he vanished, probably, Denis guessed, into one of the gardens, perhaps the garden of his own house. At any rate he left the big boys who had attempted to follow him uneasily laughing and jeering to their own Pyrrhic victory. Only a couple of nights later he heard the sweet magical sound of Lady Hogan's whistling again, obviously none the worse for his adventure. Later, when he was older, he remembered seeing him pedalling around on a carrier bicycle, a messenger boy for one of the shops in Rathmines. Those times it was only necessary to send the cook down or lift the telephone and you could have an order on your doorstep in half an hour. The Swastika laundry used to deliver its clean bundles by a horse-drawn van which made the sort of noise over the cobblestones which he imagined the old stage-coaches in Dickens used to make, but there was another way of having your washing done. You could give it at the door to the little woman who lived in a white-washed cottage actually *in* the Dodder river, on an island near the weir, and she would wash the clothes in the river and let her son trundle them back to you spotless and starched in a four-wheeled cart.

The river was much the same as it had always been and Denis often walked there. But many of the giant elms had fallen to the Dutch disease and the washerwoman's cottage was gone. An ugly new bridge with an underground crossing replaced the old twin-arched stone bridge he remembered, and at the Dartry end many of the cottages that in summer used to be smothered in roses were gone. A few were left but they were owned by city people. Boys still fished in the River Dodder, of course, and people still walked their dogs there. One day a boy who was fishing told Denis that the river was cleaner than it had ever been and his father caught a three-pound trout last week. The only fish he ever actually saw being taken out of that river were little palpitating fingerlings and usually the boy fishermen threw them back. Fishing was a pleasure he couldn't indulge in any more, and Olivia had laughed at him. What he couldn't do, or at any rate what he was not prepared to do, was either beat the fish to death with a stone or watch it slowly dying out of its element on the bank. Just before he gave up fishing for good he went a stage further. He found it increasingly difficult to bait the hook with a live worm (what had the worm done to deserve this?). As for live frogs, one March day he had watched a boy driving his hook through the fragile green body of a frog and then watched the convulsive legs which would lure the fish and finally the great pulsating eyes as the creature lay gasping among the grasses on the bank. When he was on his way back the frog was still alive and he had asked the boy to release it in return for money to buy dry flies. The boy had refused quite politely. When he saw fishermen those days he circled carefully around them, trying to concentrate his mind on something else. To be fully consistent, of course, he shouldn't eat fish which had been caught by other people, but he was a sham and he did.

This particular evening he avoided the river and finished his strolling inspection of as many good gardens as he could remember. The sun had gone down in a salmon-pink sky and there was more than a hint of approaching summer in the air as he made his way back to the apartment. In two days he would be sixty-three, April 23rd, same birthday as Shakespeare's. He had carefully avoided all mention of it to Anita and he half-hoped now that his family would forget it. When he saw the letter in the entrance hall he knew they had not. It was beautifully addressed, spaced as only Olivia and Alison knew how, and the envelope was blue, thick and handsome. He carried it doubtfully up to his apartment and fed his clamorous cats before he opened it. One settled on his shoulder and the other on his lap as he read: 'You won't be in the least surprised dear Denis to get a letter for your birthday.'

These days, when she did write, she always avoided a

conventional beginning. 'Dear Denis' was too cold and anything warmer might be indicative of what he might not welcome. So she embedded the more intimate dear Denis in the text to have it both ways. Clever, as always. He held the letter for a few moments unread in his hands, fighting the temptation to put it back in its envelope.

You won't be in the least surprised dear Denis to get a letter for your birthday. You'll even get a card as well, on the day! But I wanted to let you know in good time (I hope) that Ben and I would be thrilled if you could come over here and let us cook dinner for you on the 23rd. [Thrilled. She had never lost the schoolgirlish style of the forties.] We hope to have Alison and Colm too and she has a little surprise for you. I have another and it's this: Your son Ben has turned into a good cook, how about that? We all know about his famous desserts, but he surprised me several evenings by turning in a lovely main meal – usually pasta things which he learnt to do in Germany when he shared a flat with Italians.

This is the first time I felt it would be fair to squeeze your arm by inviting you, dear Denis, and I hope you will see your way to come. Naturally we will understand if you are not free, but it would be so lovely if you were, and we could all be together again for one evening.

Ever affectionately,

Olivia.

He put the letter back in its envelope and then put the envelope carefully under the bread bin before sitting down with an armful of cats to consider the situation. They had all, always, obsessively celebrated birthdays and every other anniversary they could think of but he didn't really see what there was to celebrate about being sixty-three and back where he started again. He was even tidier now than he had been as a boy setting himself up in his first independent apartment. Living alone was something you could organise to be agreeable. You could plan never to have a single offensive object like a thrown-off shirt or an unmade bed facing you when you got home. You could clear away and wash up as you went, always returning home to the reassurance of order. He had got used to it, and used to the delightful disruption of Friday nights. But this invitation bothered him.

Separation after a lifetime of apparently happy marriage had been a shock with which he had had to come to terms. He and Olivia had always been so different that he had grown to believe it didn't matter. They were used to one another's ways and he used to have a great affection for her. But her decision to set up on her own and physically break up his background bit by bit had been shocking and there was no other word for it. Every piece of furniture had been an agreed decision between them both. Everything had been bought in auction-rooms or in junk shops apart from the few pieces each had taken from the family home. Olivia had been unable to control her greed to possess one of these and had done battle time and again for that walnut davenport which had been his mother's pride and joy. When he finally gave in and let Olivia have it, it hurt him physically to hand it over. But it wasn't the worst thing. The worst thing was his garden, his rambling, half-wild garden which every year he dreamed into a better state, sometimes successfully. For instance, two years before the break-up he had remembered in time about the new raspberry plants. The old ones from which the canes had been cut back every autumn were so far past their best that one year their yield was only about six or seven pounds. So he had reluctantly parted with them and the canes were mature and healthy and bearing beautiful juicy berries the year the house was sold. Sometimes he imagined himself back in the hot blast of sun after a July shower, standing steaming among the prickling raspberry bushes and listening (it was a fancy of his) to their

82

ripening. He often remembered searching on a dull morning for ripe berries and finding none, and then gathering a bowlful at lunchtime to eat with Olivia. She didn't like the smell down there near the compost heap and so when the children were small he always did the picking. Later they would not be denied the pleasure, and he remembered picking raspberries with them, and their small faces running with juice which dried quickly in the sun and left them bedaubed.

Was it only the garden and his family he missed or was it Olivia? She had been a cheerful companion and a good homemaker. She had bullied him gently. She hadn't forgotten that they had been happy, although she wasn't interested in him sexually any more. But in the end she had sawn him off like a dead branch and now she wanted to celebrate his birthday with him as a sentimental gesture. Or was it? Was she perhaps bored or lonely living alone? She was in fact not living alone. Ben was with her now. Why should she invite him to dinner now of all times except it was for the reason she gave? It would be nice to do it for old time's sake. It would be a friendly family occasion and why not? Stroking a loudly purring cat with each hand, he thought seriously about it. Why not?

It was easy to get used to being alone if you were not interrupted. Fridays for him were not an interruption but part of the shape of the week, a treat like a cream bun or a walk by the river. Anita, he knew, was a strictly limited pleasure. He had trained himself to be aware that some week she would phone (being kind and polite) and make an excuse about that evening. Some week she would find her match, some young fellow her own age with whom she would start a sensible relationship unlike the fantasy of her nights with him, a man old enough to be her father. Anita in fact found him (he knew) a very useful substitute for the father she had tragically lost when she was a child of ten. They were kind to one another. It was physical, but it was not only physical. It was a sort of make-believe, cherished because of its impermanence.

But Olivia would be a very different matter. Eating again with Olivia, enjoying the exuberance of his family again with Olivia might be a danger. It was important to remember that Olivia didn't mean it. Olivia loved playing games, dramatising herself and others. She had cast them all in her next production. She would not suffer when it folded but he might. He thought about this very carefully indeed. There had been nothing about family life he hadn't liked. He liked the security and the excitement of the early days with Olivia. He had enjoyed setting up the home, finding everything they needed for it. He had loved walking down the long garden before breakfast, even in winter, and looking back at the homeliness of it, the smoke rising from the chimney-stacks, the pigeons on the roof, the current cat blinking in the kitchen window, the rattle of milk bottles out in the front which he would carry in for breakfast. In thirty years nobody else had ever carried in milk bottles, or left them out at night for that matter. He loved routines, unplugging electric gadgets, locking doors, switching off lights except for the two which burned all night. He liked to listen to his old house ticking over before he finally went to bed – the creaking lead water-pipes, the boards which always sighed when most of the heat died down, the shutters which rattled on windy nights. He liked to see that everything was safe before he went to bed himself.

Then when there were children it was even better. Olivia would always be tired after the day, always eager for bed. She'd smile at him over her shoulder – 'You'll tuck them in as usual, won't you love?' – and he'd always nod happily. There was nothing he liked better than tiptoeing in and checking that they were all right for the night. From early babyhood Alison would hardly stir. Thumb in her mouth, hair curling all over the pillow, she would sometimes sigh and smile when he tightened the clothes about her but never waken. Ben was different. His room would be a litter of strewn toys scattered, it seemed, at the last desperate moment before sleep. For years

Ben had had to be lifted at night and placed on the pot, otherwise his bed would be wet in the morning. The bed was always in a chaotic state anyway and Ben would be lying diagonally across it, bedclothes unhitched and rolled into a ball. They had evolved a way of tying the bedclothes on but this could only be done at the last moment. Ben's hands would often be tightened into fists, his teeth grinding. If by any chance he was wakened at this stage he would cry causelessly for half an hour before dropping exhausted into a shallow sleep again. This had lasted for years and sometimes Denis found himself wondering how the grown Ben slept now. Often it would be two o'clock before he got to bed himself in the old days and by then Olivia would be sleeping like Alison, deeply and tranquilly, and he would crawl carefully into bed for fear of waking her.

It had taken a while to break those old routines. He didn't really know how he would react if for one evening his mind became full of his family again, their voices, their touching hands, the resurrection of the old jokes, the old passwords. Very like a whale. How had that begun? He remembered it was Ben himself who had established it and its specific connotation. Each and all of them said 'Very like a whale' at times as though the whole world should understand. What in fact did it mean? It meant not only an unwillingness for conflict. In the family connotation it also meant something somewhat unsatisfactory. 'How did the day go?' Olivia might say, and the reply would be 'Very like a whale'. Ben himself used it in addition to connote something that went according to plan although the plan might not have been a very good one in the first place. It was in fact impossible to explain all this to an outsider and he wondered how Colm for instance would be able to stand such a semantically interlocked family as theirs had always been.

It was the thought of Colm's presence that finally decided Denis he might take a chance on it. It would after all not be a family evening as it always had been because Colm and Alison were now another family with no doubt their own mythologies. He gently brushed away the cats and they went twining warmly in and out of his legs as he found notepaper and began to write. She hadn't squeezed his arm by phoning so he'd write to her too.

April 18th, Monday

Dear Olivia,

What can I do but thank you for your letter and your kind invitation even if I have some misgivings about accepting it. I do not as you know find change easy and I did not have much choice about the most revolutionary change of my life. I've come to terms with that in my own way and I quite enjoy my new routines now. I feel I should prudently refuse to join you all and ignore my birthday which would be the nicest present I could give myself. However your letter is so kind that I find this difficult. I am a little apprehensive about how we may all react to one another when we are all together again after several years but nevertheless expect me at 7.30 for 8.00 on Wednesday as you suggest. Any other reply would be cowardice.

Affection reciprocated,
Denis.

It seemed to him smug when read over and quite ungracious, but he sealed it anyhow and went out with it to the letterbox at the corner, VR for Victoria Regina. Underneath its green paint was the dear Queen's insignia and the crown for ever embedded there. Patriotic green though it was, that piece of street furniture was red underneath and it touched him to remember that it had been receiving letters of all kinds into its jaws for more than a hundred years. When he had posted this particular letter he wished for a moment that he had it back again, as people long dead must have done over and over again.

86

8

Colm and Alison were having trouble with the au pair again. Now that the weather had improved so dramatically they couldn't understand why Monique still slumped indoors and had stopped attending her classes. Even a walk by the river with the children was something she had to be practically beaten into doing. She still watched the post obsessively every morning so it was obviously not going so well with the boy friend in Paris. There were advantages of course in the evenings, because even an unexpected invitation to go out could be accepted. Monique seemed positively to welcome an evening alone with the sleeping children. Her heavy dark face would attempt a smile if Alison apologised for going out with Colm two nights running. She would shrug 'Mais ça ne fait rien' and Alison would reply gently, 'English please, Monique. You're here to learn, remember.'

'I do not mind to stay in,' Monique would reply. 'I read, I watch television, I like.'

'Why don't you come with us to the theatre on Friday as a little treat? I'll ask Ben to babysit – it was Colm who suggested this and I'd love you to come.'

'Thank you. D'accord,' Monique would say. She seemed to like rousing herself to go out with them, but not alone. They couldn't understand it.

On the night of her father's birthday Alison left the French girl a box of her favourite marrons glacés to solve her own conscience because they had been out several times already that week. Monique smiled her slow unappealing smile as she took the box, and then made what for her was a major effort.

'Enjoy it,' she said to Alison and Colm and they talked about her most of the way to Monkstown. Colm thought he ought to drop into the language school and find out what her problems there might be. She got frequent letters from her parents and a regular monthly cheque to cover the fees. They felt responsible for her and wished they could see the slightest progress. But they forgot about her in the immediate prospect of seeing Olivia and Denis together again. Alison felt apprehensive and said so.

'But you yourself wanted to arrange something like this, didn't you?'

'On neutral ground, Colm,' Alison said firmly. 'In *our* house it would have been quite different. I'm not at all sure Mother's flat is the right setting.'

'Look, if your father agreed to come it will be all right,' said Colm easily. 'He's a nice sensible man. If he couldn't take this thing he'd have said no, wouldn't he?'

'Not if he felt he was obliged to get us all together when the opportunity presented itself.'

'Stop worrying and look to your left over there.'

Walking along swinging his arms was Alison's father, a man who had hated cars all his life and now rejoiced in not having to run one. His stride seemed cheerful and confident but he climbed agreeably into the back seat when they pulled into the pavement.

'Happy birthday, Denis,' they both said together and he grinned at them.

'Don't you think rationally it's time we forgot about my birthday?'

'Never,' Alison said. 'Birthdays are for celebrating at *any* age. Would you like to open up the parcel on the back seat now?'

'Later,' Denis said, 'but thank you very much.' He sounded pleased and amused at the elaborately wrapped parcel which had an orchid stuck into the purple string.

'This I'll wear,' he decided and Alison handed him a pin from her lapel.

'It was wrapped up in plastic like an Easter egg,' Alison said. 'It took me five minutes to open up and just stick it there.'

'Simple of itself,' her father said. 'A perfect buttonhole for a silly day. Reminds me of the only serious temptation of my life. On the banks of a small muddy river in Monaghan once I found four wild orchids with tiger-striped leaves. Wanted there and then to dig up two at least with my penknife and bring them home to the garden.'

'But you didn't,' Alison rightly guessed.

'I didn't. But I've been thinking of them ever since, you know, off and on. Of course they mightn't have grown. So I tell myself. It's a long way from a muddy river in Monaghan to a Rathgar garden.'

'Next time I go home I'll dig up some for you,' Colm promised. His parents had a farm in Fermanagh. 'They're common as primroses around the lakelands. You could try them.'

'Thanks but I've no garden now,' Denis said, and Colm felt stricken suddenly.

'A window-box would do splendidly,' Alison chipped quickly in. 'That way you could control the moisture. Keep them as damp as you liked. Look, here we are.' Colm edged into the drive of a house set well back from the road, with a shelter belt of trees to the back of it.

When they rang the bell, Olivia's voice spoke from the intercom. 'Who is it, please?' 'It's us,' said Alison and they heard Olivia responding, 'How lovely! Welcome!' Then they could push open the door. Olivia was waiting for them outside the door of her own flat. She was wearing a fine dark blue and gold Indian cotton dress with full sleeves and a fringed hem.

Her arms in the big sleeves were stretched wide to welcome them all, but she lingered over the hug for Denis and then held him out like a prize exhibit to examine.

'Many happy returns, love,' she said, and kissed him again.

Inside there was a big log fire and flowers everywhere. Ben was in the kitchen but he came out with a bottle of champagne and a big smile. Olivia had arranged the glasses when they all came back after throwing their coats on her bed. The cork exploded like a gunshot and showered Ben's hands with champagne.

'Happy birthday, Denis.'

'Many happy returns, Dad.'

Denis felt shy and found it a little difficult to respond. 'Denis,' they all said then and sipped, and he drank half his own glass quite rapidly as soon as they had lowered theirs. Knowing Olivia he felt there must be something behind this evening but he was content to let it take its course.

She was exceptionally nice to him. She didn't ask him how he was getting on or attempt to lead him on a Cook's tour of her elegant apartment. She sat on the floor and talked about the time Alison had her birthday in Bettystown during the holidays when she was seven and nobody had remembered to buy the cake.

'You decorated a fairy cake, Ben,' Alison remembered. 'You stuck smarties all over it and a stump of candle in the middle. After the "Happy birthday to you" bit I cut dolls' slices with a penknife and I remember wondering why anybody ever had a big cake when it always tasted so awful anyway.'

'We did a bit better for you tonight, Denis – wait till you see. It was Ben's suggestion and it worked out nicely, I think.'

'What's for dinner?' Alison wanted to know.

'Your father's favourite meal – what else?' Olivia answered and Denis found himself struggling to remember what his favourite meal might have been during that time which already had receded so completely that he regarded the people gathered around him almost as kind and agreeable strangers.

'Don't you remember?' Olivia had been quick to interpret the look on his face. 'It was the Tuesday dinner in the old days.'

'Braised garlic steak with mushrooms,' Alison said, pointing her nose in the direction of the kitchen, and so it was.

Denis attempted to wear a smile which would satisfy them all, but it was difficult. Even the ritual of spending hours cooking a large meal for five people seemed bizarre to him now. A meal could so easily be put together from trays of this and that in the delicatessen. He wasn't ungrateful but it all seemed folly to him now. Not their all being here together. That was unexpectedly pleasant and even quite easy. It became easier as the evening wore on and Alison went mysteriously to the kitchen to bring in her contribution to the feast. It seems she had left it here the previous evening, a large elaborately iced birthday cake in yellow and white, with sixty-three candles blazing away. That at least was not according to custom, so they all laughed at it. According to custom there was always one fat candle for adults to represent thirty, forty, fifty or sixty years with the remainder of the age made up in small birthday candles. But this must have taken several boxes of candles and a lot of trouble for Alison to achieve. Olivia sprang to quench all the lights and she even blew out the table candles. There it was, the symbol of his old age simmering away there in a cheerful blaze, the supposedly non-drip candles dissolving onto the icing, the HAPPY BIRTHDAY DADDY, so elegantly written in sugar, already blurring in the heat. As they had done for at least twenty-five years they all sang 'Happy birthday to you' and clapped loudly as he attempted to blow out all sixty-three candles together. He noticed help from the far side of the table from Olivia and indeed the candles did die all together, leaving only the firelight and the laughter and the kisses. It would have been embarrassing except for the firelight. Later, as the cake was handed around, Olivia decided to light only the dinner candles, so he knew there was no way they could be sure that his cheeks were flushed and his eyes itchy. They all remembered other birthdays. Alison reminded them of the time she fought one of her guests on the doorstep for a going-home present which she coveted and Olivia once again reminded them of her recurring nightmare when Ben and Alison were small children.

'I'm just looking out through the front window happy that I've got through most of the day's work and I notice this little girl coming in the front gate under the trees. She's all dressed up and she has a brightly wrapped parcel dangling from one wrist, and then she's joined along the garden path by another little girl in a party dress with a parcel and then by a boy with slicked-down hair and I tear my own hair and I say, "Jesus no! It's not today . . . it can't be!" – and it is. It's the day of Alison's birthday party and all her friends are confidently arriving and their parents won't collect them for five hours and I've forgotten! There's nothing ready. Not a cocktail sausage in the house. Not a rice-krispie cake cooked. Not a single wrapped-up toy for Pass the Parcel. I wake up screaming.'

They all gasp and laugh, as they always did, and Denis gets the message, or (he concedes) maybe unkindly believes he does. Olivia is telling them how sleeping and waking she has always had the care of them all on her mind. He knew it was true, just as an earlier nightmare about leaving a small bundle of baby in the corner of a pub was true. That was soon after Alison was born. He wondered now if Olivia regretted anything, breaking up definitively what she had built with such determination and care over so many years. In the middle of all the chatter he found himself silent, a shellfish left behind by the tide. Olivia, before he was aware of it, had noticed and winkled him out into the hall where she smiled at him in the kindest possible way.

'I promise you, Denis, that little token parcel tonight is not your birthday present. Come in till I show you. He followed her out into a bedroom that could not possibly have been anybody else's but Olivia's and she led him to the davenport that had been part of his earliest memories.

'That', said Olivia, 'is one of the lousiest things I've ever done in my whole life. I should never have pressed you to let me have it and it's going back to you tomorrow.'

'Nonsense,' he said, actually blushing. 'You were welcome as I told you to anything you fancied. It's over and done with – finished. It's yours. I'd forgotten it. How well it looks over there.'

'I will not be baulked over this.' Olivia smiled, and he knew, of course, that she wouldn't. 'Will it suit you to be at home between eleven and twelve tomorrow morning?'

'If you insist, I'll phone them at the office.'

'I do insist. And it's even arranged with CIE. The stupid people couldn't promise it for today which of course is when I wanted it delivered. Thank you, Denis, for allowing me to undo something truly selfish. Your mother's favourite piece from the old house. You often told me – it wasn't as if I didn't know.'

'Sometime I'll find you another,' he found himself saying, hating all this, only wanting it over and done with because it was so typical of Olivia. Greedy as a child (as Alison over that going-home parcel destined for her friend long ago) she frequently suffered pangs of remorse of which he was now the victim. He walked over to the window and looked down at the lights of Dublin like low stars over her garden. She followed him, not answering when he remarked on the splendour of her view. He knew she was smiling behind his back.

'Does it ever amuse you, Denis, honestly, to be the age we are – well I've only a few years to go – and yet not feel any different from being thirty or even twenty?'

'I feel quite different.'

'Oh you know perfectly well what I mean! When we were twenty we thought people of thirty were old – settled and in a way finished. Then when we were thirty we thought that way about people in their forties, and then fifties, and all the time ageing was part of the process of other people's lives, not ours. Now you're sixty plus and I'm not far from it myself and still it's not old age, or even maturity. I still feel the idiot I always was, about some things. All those years and no more real confidence or being sure about anything.' (Olivia not sure about anything?)

He had denied it, but he knew what she meant, all the same. It was what divided him from Anita who knew he was safe and elderly and utterly dependable. His own uncertainty about coming here tonight was no different from the uncertainty of youth. They had lived virtually all their lives together, he and Olivia, and now it was over, yet she was still the only person who moved in his own orbit. She too had learned that the confidence of maturity didn't exist. She knew you are what you were at twenty or even younger. Only the body changed, and he suddenly realised that hers hadn't changed all that much. She was still healthy and intact and she still had the quick swooping movements of youth. Her face was finely lined when you really looked into it, but it was the same face, not a fat face instead of a thin face, not a red face instead of a rosy one, not (in her case) a yellow face instead of a brown face. She was Olivia still, with all the steamroller security for which he had married her and all the old maddening determination to ignore facts.

'I'm so happy you came, Denis,' she said kneeling beside him on the window-seat. 'I don't think I could have borne it if you'd said no. I want us to be friends.'

'How could we ever be anything else?'

'Oh, there are friends and friends,' she said impatiently. 'Friends you never see. Friends you wish you saw less of. Friends who send Christmas cards. Friends who write long letters once in a while. They are the friends who won't accept that people change and grow out of one another. But we did all our growing together, Denis, and together we watched our children grow up. If we were ever to become the sort of friends who exchange Christmas cards I think I'd die.'

He was baffled, even after all these years of knowing her strong resistance to facts. It was she who had ended the marriage and set up house briefly with somebody else.

'It's true, we grew up together, Olivia,' he said gently. 'But I never could understand you. I don't now.'

'Think about it.' She tightened a hand on his arm. 'Think about it and you will. Meanwhile let me show you my latest craze.'

She led him to the concealed staircase and switched on a white globe that hung at the top of it. His knees creaked as he followed her quick strides up the stairs. It was the sort of small pretty spiral staircase that young people fitted nowadays to make full use of attic space. This was precisely what Olivia had done.

He was out of breath when he reached the top, quite unfit to do justice to the explosion of colour that greeted him. There was a small loom in the far corner under a skylight and there were rainbow lengths of loosely woven wool everywhere. They hung from several old towel racks (which he recognised as surely as he had the davenport) and from larger racks fitted along the wall. She swooped on a piece of cobweb wool the colour of blackberries and draped it over his shoulders.

'For your cats,' she said, kissing him suddenly on the cheek. 'They'll love it and if they tear it to shreds I'll make you another.'

'Thank you very much, Olivia,' he said.

It was impossible not to respond, to praise the unusual blackberry shade of the dye, to express admiration for her industry when he learned that (of course) no commercial process had been used to achieve it but only a large pan of simmering blackberries which she had picked herself last September. From this revelation was a short jump back to the childhood of Ben and Alison, the back-at-school weekends when they had gone to Killinarden where the juiciest berries were to be found. That place was a housing estate now, its sloping fields of brambles all bulldozed away.

'Where will Alison take the children when they grow a bit?' Olivia wondered, as though it were an immediate problem. 'Wicklow, I suppose. I gathered my blackberries last year as far away as Glenmalure.'

'I shouldn't wonder if Alison could find splendid berries a stone's throw away from her home along the Dodder,' Denis said. 'The future really presents no problem for blackberry pickers. The problem is to keep the brambles out of one's garden.' He felt a little bored.

'We had a good life, Denis, hadn't we, all those years?'

'No regrets,' he said lightly.

'Really?'

'Really. Thank you very much for this extremely handsome cat blanket. You are probably right that it will be appreciated, especially when I tell them it's handwoven and dyed with real blackberries.'

The humour was heavy and not entirely kind. Olivia looked dissatisfied as he removed the pretty cobwebby thing and folded it over one arm. She urged him ahead of her down the stairs and then regretted it as she followed his slow careful progress. She began to say something but took it back again as they returned to the fire. There was not a great deal of the evening left. Alison had already begun to worry about the children. She worried about her parents when she and Colm were driving home after having deposited Denis at his hall door.

'How did you think it went?'

'I don't know.' Colm seemed to be thinking it out as he spoke. 'Sticky at times, especially towards the end, and then there were times when they seemed entirely easy and natural together.'

'But they weren't, you see. There was nothing natural about

96

them tonight at all.'

'She still obviously feels a little guilty. I mean, wasn't she the one who broke a long and successful marriage, not Denis?'

'When Mother felt guilty was always when you had to look out,' Alison said uneasily. 'I didn't like tonight at all, and I'd like to sound out Ben about it.'

Her thoughts were so completely elsewhere that the shock when she let herself into the house was all the greater. The side door leading to the conservatory and the garden was wide open. There was an empty whiskey bottle and broken glass on the floor. Heart pounding, Alison raced upstairs to check on the children. She found the baby deeply asleep as she had left him, and her daughter missing. The child had not gone far. She was curled up asleep on Monique's bed and the girl had one arm around her. Monique's own eyes were wide open but unmoving and blood was trickling down from a deep cut on her forehead. One of her cheeks was dark red and puffy. Tomorrow it would be a bruise.

Colm came racing upstairs after he had put away the car to find Alison carefully carrying her daughter back to bed, still fast asleep. He knelt down beside the French girl and took her hand which began to shake violently as he held it. Alison came back with a damp facecloth.

'Thank God the children are all right,' she said to Colm, who went immediately downstairs to phone the guards and the doctor. When he returned, Monique's face was still turned rigidly away from Alison's questioning and Colm knelt down again and gently turned the shaking shoulders so that the girl was facing them.

'Tell us what happened, Monique, there's a good girl.'

Alison bent instinctively and kissed her as she would one of the children. 'Please, Monique, we only want to know what happened. Nobody wants to blame you.'

The damaged eyes opened again, full of tears this time. 'No police,' she said.

'Now look, that's not reasonable. You know perfectly well this *is* a matter for the guards. Nobody wants to blame you, Monique,' she said again, and Alison felt helpless, a strange sensation for her. Her mind suddenly turned to the unknown, well-organised people who were the girl's parents, who sent money so regularly and wrote fortnightly letters. They had sent their daughter trustfully away to further her education and somehow she and Colm had disastrously failed to keep their side of the bargain. Monique had learned little English, had been sulky it's true but faithful in her care of the children, and now she was lying injured and shattered in what she had every right to regard as her own home. Alison was used to being in control of every situation. This one was beyond her and her sense of guilt was heightened by the realisation that she had known all along that the girl was unhappy and had done nothing about it. Rather had she unethically taken advantage of the unusual amount of freedom the girl's lack of a social life had given her. Her mind took a painful jump forward to her own daughter many years ahead, maybe alone and uncared for in Paris. She clung to Colm as she had not done for a long time, not since the night before young Olivia was born. They stood with arms fastened around one another, still in Monique's room, waiting for the insanely cheerful carillon of the doorbell.

'It will be all right,' Colm whispered. 'It isn't our fault, remember that. Any of it.' When the bell sounded he went at once downstairs and she took a last look at the children. They were still asleep and she should have been grateful. Instead she found herself wondering for the first time what horrors the four-year-old might have witnessed and she began to shiver as Colm called her and she went slowly downstairs after a last look at the clenched hands and the averted face of the girl on the bed. She shook hands dazedly with the guard as though this were an ordinary social call.

'Shouldn't you wait until the doctor has seen Monique?' she

asked. 'I'm sure he won't be long.'

'We both think Garda Henneghan should see her first,' Colm said. 'You wait down here, Alison, to let the doctor in. By the sound of him the poor man was in his bed. It may be a few minutes before he gets here.'

'Don't worry, mam,' the young guard said with a paternal expression on his broad face. 'I won't startle the young lady.'

'She's been startled enough already,' Alison said. 'Be gentle with her, won't you?'

'I will, so,' the guard said. 'If we could just go up to her now, sir? Don't clear away that broken glass yet, mam.' With a childish impulse of which she was hardly aware Alison sat on the last step of the stairs and hugged her knees as she listened to the feet moving above her. She heard the two voices of the men, but not a sound from Monique. She imagined the injured face averted once again, the puffy eyes closed, the hands clenched. Rape? In the presence of the four-year-old? Had the rapist been known or unknown to the girl? Jumping up, Alison made a quick check on the few pieces of plate and silver they owned. The plate was untouched, the silver gone. Nothing else was disturbed. Just the smashed glass and the empty whiskey bottle. The carillon sounded again at the door and she went to let in the doctor, a fragile, elderly man well-known in the district for his way with sick children. As always he looked impeccably neat in the silver-grey suit as though this were an ordinary morning call. Alison shook hands with him and thanked him for coming out at this hour. His smile was kind but it vanished when he heard the story of the au pair girl.

'I'll go up at once and have a look at her.'

Colm met the doctor at the foot of the stairs, shook hands and indicated the guard on the landing.

'We are dealing, I think, with a very frightened young woman in a foreign country,' Dr Lindsay said. 'I'd be obliged if you would wait downstairs while I examine her. I'll give you a full report of her condition.'

'Right you are, Doctor,' the young guard agreed at once. 'We couldn't get a word out of her ourselves, could we, sir?'

'Give me ten minutes, gentlemen.'

Colm went to make coffee and Alison sat down again on the last step. She watched in some fascination as the empty whiskey bottle was finger-printed, together with two large pieces of the broken glass. She reported the stolen silver with a feeling of total unreality, as though she had stepped straight out of her father's birthday party into a nightmare. How long ago was it? It seemed to be days ago. Colm put a cup of coffee into her hands and they wondered if they should ring Paris or wait until the morning. It seemed a long time before footsteps sounded on the stairs again. The young guard came first, shaking his head as he showed them a long, thick finger of broken glass with blood half-dried on its surface. Alison rushed for the bathroom as Garda Henneghan wrapped the weapon in a tissue before folding it into his pocket. Dazed, Alison watched the hand-basin receiving the cup of coffee she had just drunk. Dr Lindsay took a while longer to appear.

'I'll look in again in the morning,' he said to Colm. 'And, officer, on my way I'll leave a written report at the station. I've given Monique a sedative which should allow her a rest until morning. Don't worry,' he ended with a kind look at Colm and Alison. 'She's young and in a couple of months she'll know it's not the end of the world. She's been badly shocked and in my opinion she had another problem which I'll specify in my report, but I don't think we should add to her misery by admitting her to hospital. I'll bring a letter with me tomorrow for her parents,' he said to Alison. 'Her injuries are fortunately not serious but obviously the parents must know. She may need psychiatric care for a short time. Rape is always traumatic.'

'Did she know him?' Colm asked faintly.

It was the guard who answered.

'If he's the prize thug that I think he is (since Mrs O'Dea told me about the missing silver) I'd say she didn't know him – on the other hand,' he covered his retreat, 'I don't know the girl or her habits.' He coughed, leaving a slight disturbance in the air. 'I'll proceed with trying to collect evidence against the party I have in mind and if I succeed we'll take him in. It's not easy to pin down the gentry I have in mind, so it isn't. There's a nest of them in it, but I think I know which of them would carry out tonight's ugly business.'

Both policeman and doctor politely refused the coffee Colm offered and inside five minutes he and Alison were alone again in the living-room of their violated dolls' house, not really able to take in the events of the long crazy night. What was the 'other problem' Monique might have, Alison wondered. Pregnancy? They discussed the remoteness of this possibility until nearly morning, and when the infant upstairs at last wailed for food they actually welcomed the sound of everyday life returning. It was half-past four and already tomorrow.

9

The first time Ben invited Anita into his flat was a few weeks after he had found it, a gaunt attic approached by a crumbling staircase in a house whose race was run. In front it was shored up by buttresses roughly made because the last tenants believed that the front walls were in danger of falling into the street. Most of these tenants had been rehoused, except one old man who shared the basement with a senile dog and dozens of rats. He refused to leave and was being supported for the time being by an organisation dedicated to the aged. Mr Coyle had been born here, had passed all his adult life here with a mother who had recently died, and Mr Coyle intended eventually to die here. The relief organisation had searched for some responsible young person who might enjoy the attic flat and look in on Mr Coyle every other day before climbing the ruined staircase after work. The rent was nominal and the house was quite convenient to the school so Ben used it as an excuse to move out of his mother's flat. She took it very well and he saw her most Sundays for dinner.

The day Anita called to visit the old man in the course of her work was one of the last days of April when summer seemed a distinct possibility. There were no trees in this dying district but a bloom of pinkish light lay everywhere over the decayed brick suggesting how this square may have looked when only the rich lived here. Around four o'clock every afternoon the fanlights were warmed by filtered sunlight coming through the broken stained-glass windows at the back of the hall. To Anita's amazement Mr Coyle's buttressed house even looked welcoming that day because somebody had actually cleaned the brasses and watered two pots of geraniums at the top of the steps. Mr Coyle insisted louder than ever that this was a grand little place, so it was, even better since the new tenant moved in upstairs and nobody was going to drive him out of it into no new flat. Anita spent a fruitless hour talking to him on behalf of Dublin Corporation and in the end he escaped from her out into the area where he began sweeping rubbish to end the conversation. He waved his brush to the young man passing by who in fact did not pass by and whom she suddenly recognised. Ben answered her shouted greeting in friendly fashion and invited her up with him for coffee. She was getting nowhere with Mr Coyle anyhow so she thankfully made her farewells and ran up the steps to where Denis's son was grinning down at her.

'So you are the cleaner of brasses that I half-suspected Mr Coyle was inventing? The new tenant?'

'I suppose you could call me that but I've been here a few weeks. Come in, Anita.' His smile exactly and movingly recalled his father's as he fitted his key into the lock and let her into a pungent smell of urine that lingered in the hall and on the crumbling staircase despite (Ben said) his efforts to get rid of it. Open doors sagging on their hinges revealed gaunt abandoned rooms where large families had once been reared. Decayed net curtains still clung to some of the windows. Piles of rubbish and broken furniture indicated futile efforts to make a clean sweep of leaving. A baby's pram with three wheels stood crookedly on one of the landings, but as the two mounted carefully because of missing steps it became obvious that Ben had made efforts to improve his own immediate environment. Up there the entrances to abandoned apartments had been closed off and a window-sill was adorned with another pot of genaniums beginning to bloom. Nothing obviously could be done about the pervasive smell of decay but when Ben opened the door of his attic the smell was different, a combination of spices and new paint. Anita laughed and ran to the window.

'I like it,' she said. 'I like it. That's a bird's eye view that people buying new apartments are happy to pay the extra few thousands for.'

However, his most immediate bird's eye view was of another house like this across the road whose entire walls had been removed to be replaced as far as eye level with a red and white hoarding for the safety of passers-by. Above it were the tiers of front rooms and exposed chimney-breasts, wallpaper torn and flapping in the breeze, the remains of electric fittings and lampshades, and (almost at a level with the attic) a perfectly good red kitchen chair drawn up to a table. One had the impression that the last person to sit down there had been taken by surprise. Beyond all this desolation were the docklands, distant masts, Poolbeg Lighthouse, the glittering blue bay closed off at one arm by Howth Head and at the other by the wooded rise of Killiney Hill. Low above the spires and office blocks of the old city in between was this pinkening of the very air which was caused by approaching summer struggling with city pollution.

'I like it,' Anita said again, 'but I couldn't live here.'

'You haven't been asked,' Ben said crisply and enjoyed her laugh. He looked with her eyes at the clean bare boards (he would sand and wax them if he stayed), the beanbag, the red Indian rug, the two kitchen chairs, the table he had rescued from downstairs and cleaned up, the orange boxes arranged like bookshelves, the blue sleeping bag in the far corner with a recently purchased anglepoise red lamp above it, and a Klimt poster of prisoners behind it.

'There *is* a bedroom,' he said, following her glance, 'but I prefer to sleep here. It's warmer – gets the sun all day long –

and besides there's less difference between night and day when you sleep on the floor.'

'This is a good thing?'

'A very good thing. The shock is less when you surface every morning.'

She laughed again and flopped down very unconcernedly on his beanbag.

'Coffee?'

'Lovely,' she said, reaching out for his fat volume of Pound which had travelled around with him in his rucksack. He was amused to note how well-reared she had been, not presuming to follow him into a kitchen which might not be fit for presentation (but was in fact), not taking it for granted she could rush in to look at his bedroom which had been cleaned but still looked pretty grim. It was at this point as he prepared to filter his Bewley's coffee that his similarity to both his parents and even to Alison struck him for the first time. Squalor, although he had courted it, did not come naturally to him. His impulse was to make order out of chaos wherever he found it. During his time abroad, he had fought down the impulse, conquered it at times, particularly with Julie's help. But it always came back. With disgust he faced the truth that if he stayed here, a doomed slumland attic would end up looking a little like Alison's place.

Anita as she welcomed the coffee looked quite at home. He supposed she was used to adapting instantly to different surroundings – she wouldn't be much good as a social worker otherwise.

'You're so like your father,' she said, when they were seated with their coffee cups at opposite sides of the beanbag. 'I don't suppose it's ever occurred to you?'

'Frequently, on the contrary. But I have a well cultivated mean streak in me that he lacks.'

She thought about this for a moment and obviously decided to ignore it.

'My own father was drowned when I was ten,' Anita offered. 'In a way I suppose I miss him still.'

'So you found a father figure in straight Freudian style?'

She was quite equal to this challenge. 'Nothing is ever quite so simple and well you know it. I never before continued to like anybody after I got to know him, as a matter of fact. I always said *no* to myself very soon after meeting a vaguely fancied man and then *yes*, but it always came back to *no* again. Only Denis seems to get better the better I know him.'

'I had hoped to interest you professionally in some of my problems,' Ben said with a smile he hoped took the harm out of it.

'Please try,' she said, sipping her coffee with composure. This was clearly going to be a quite interesting afternoon.

'Well, we're trying to build a swimming pool at the school to give some sort of focal point for the summer. Of course in this area there's no such thing as going away for a holiday.'

She agreed. 'Except, that is, for the very old who are looked after by the Vincent de Paul and the very young.'

He nodded. 'Trouble is we have almost no money. It's not like the sort of school where you can ask the parents for regular "voluntary subscriptions" but there have been voluntary subscriptions all the same. *Really* voluntary.'

Anita looked incredulous, and he laughed.

'No, not money. But for instance the father of a desperate character called Luke arrived one afternoon with a load of blue tiles that he said might look nice and warm as a lining for the pool.'

'So you didn't enquire too closely where he might have acquired them?'

'Exactly. Then in the early days we got in the same fashion a few loads of cement blocks and a lot of voluntary help from the bigger fellows and quite a few of the girls.' He paused and when she looked up at him she saw that this period of cooperation was probably a good time for him. Proof he could carry them along. She knew the feeling. 'We had the foundations properly dug and partly laid when I came in one morning to find about half a ton of rubbish tipped into the site – obviously deliberately from a truck. It meant a lot of work but we got over that and we were ready to start again in ten days. Just before I moved into this flat we had the concrete base and walls in and we were at the stage of waterproofing all this with mastic – next stage blue tiles – when a new calamity hit us. But why don't we walk over there and I'll show you when you've finished your coffee?'

'Love to.'

It was only five minutes walk away from the house but, watching his face again, she saw how it had changed: crestfallen as though all this were being seen for the first time. It was difficult to imagine how the half-made swimming pool could have been damaged to this extent. Huge cracks ran diagonally across it. An ancient and extremely heavy iron bath had been filled with rocks and dropped from some height onto one corner – something mechanical must have been used for that piece of destruction alone. The bath had sunk through the concrete and lodged itself in the foundations. It was difficult to imagine how this forlorn mess could ever be a blue-tiled swimming pool full of happy kids this coming summer. She had voiced her doubts but Ben wasn't interested.

'Look,' he said, 'see that wrecked car over near the school gate? *That* was in the pool yesterday. Some of my fellows, God knows how, are already trying to make a clearance. The crowd who did this destruction, whoever they are, don't matter, they'll soon see it's useless. But what I want to know is what extra grants might be available for an amenity such as this? The Department of Education won't help any more, nor will local government.'

'I think the answer is ANCO,' she said after thinking a few minutes. 'You might be able to get this through as a suitable project. I might even be able to help there, but I can't promise anything.'

'I don't want promises. But even the possibility of help entitles you to a drink. Come and I'll show you the most uncomfortable pub you've ever sat in.'

'I probably know it.'

In fact she did not. It was on the corner of a partly demolished street and it looked like a fortress, laced with barbed wire above the metal security doors which would be dropped into position after closing time. Inside, it smelled strongly of disinfectant, almost like a hospital except that you could smell the stale spilled Guinness too. A room beyond the bar was loud with video machines and young voices. Where until quite recently an old mahogany counter had stood with shelving to match there was a plastic surface full of cracks, broken at the edges, and the wall seats were of ragged green plastic. A coven of old men played cards in the corner and the curate saluted Ben civilly, if a little uneasily. Beyond there where the noise was were a dozen under-age drinkers at five o'clock in the afternoon. In another corner by himself a fat young man in a pinstripe suit studied racing form. He returned to his newspaper after one sharp glance in their direction.

'If you examined his concealed pockets you'd find ten-packs,' Anita whispered when Ben set a glass of lager before her, and he nodded agreement. The man was as well-known to the police as to Ben and Anita but he had never been caught pushing heroin because his dealers were children about nine or ten years of age and they were everywhere. Despite the smell and the discomfort of this pub, Anita enjoyed the company of Ben who shared with her the intimate knowledge of this lost centre of the city. Her evenings with his father were fantasy, warmly looked forward to and enjoyed, but this man of her own age belonged to the real world she knew. Before his own glass had been emptied Ben felt suddenly that getting to know her was inevitable since the night he had slept in her bed knowing he lay between the same covers that had shaped themselves to her body the night before. The sexual response was not something he had welcomed or even acknowledged until now, but when he cooked for her for the first time that evening it all seemed very simple. They lit candles because the electricity had been cut off long ago and she offered him her body as naturally as though it were a dessert fruit. The breast to which she guided his hand through the opened shirt was in fact small and firm as an apple, and as cool to the lips. He said so before searching with his tongue to open the erect nipple and she lay laughing about Eden with him on his sleeping bag, peeling him garment by garment before he opened another button of hers. Eventually he made love to her coldly and guiltily, taking her quickly once again with a resurgence he wondered at, and he wondered too at the way she didn't mind the cold-bloodedness of it at all but curved up like a fish to drink the tears that catapulted out of his eyes the second time.

10

When Monique arrived in Dun Laoire the strolling crowds had been reduced to the odd dog-owner setting out purposefully for the lighthouse, pet at heel and, along the pier, two or three fishermen casting out their lines. There was no sign of the friend whom Alison had encouraged her to meet for this walk. The sky arching over the harbour was peacock blue and cloudless with a faint thickening of light at the skyline to suggest that darkness was probably an hour or so away.

She waited for twenty minutes, enjoying the slight breeze, even enjoying the feeling that she was too thinly clad. She seemed to spend most of her life feeling too hot, too restricted, even trapped during the past year. It was a rare piece of enterprise on her part to come out here to meet a girl from her language class. She had done so only because, if she had not, Alison would joke again about a plan to walk her out like a dog on summer evenings. Recently Colm and Alison had given up trying to make her go home. They knew she had reason to hate Dublin but they had begun to understand that she couldn't even think of Paris without shrinking further still inside her shell. It had been a fight with the last of her energy to persuade them not to tell her parents about the rape. Looking back, she couldn't imagine where she had found the strength, but she had. She remembered her circling arguments. 'They are people with problems of their own, many problems and soon their marriage will be over. There is nothing they can do for me, but they will suffer to learn this. Please. No I wish to stay. No I am not afraid any more. To care for the children and to learn much English is what I wish to do. I have been lazy but this is over. Over. Over.'

Monique watched a man landing a mackerel, watched the rainbow colours fade as it flapped out the last of its life on the stone pier. Over. She had realised quite suddenly after the rape that she didn't want to use heroin any more. She had made a quite easy decision after weeks of not having had enough to make much difference anyhow. Had it not been for Philippe she wouldn't ever have started fixing in the first place. It was a shared experience that ensured magic hours away from school and away from her unhappy parents' flat in St Cloud, Philippe had told her that it was the most beautiful buzz in the world, better than skiing with perfect skill down the champions' slope at St Moritz, better than orgasm. Gods, said Philippe, the old Greek Gods felt as we feel at the needle's first kiss. 'Je t'embrasse,' he had said, emptying the first needle into her vein, but he had lied to her. She couldn't understand the panic and the sickness after what had been promised, but he had laughed at her. 'A lover must be wooed,' he had said. 'Plus tard voyons.' He was right of course but that hadn't lasted long either. Philippe himself had become less of a lover. His desire seemed to be concentrated in his veins. When he fed it and threw away the needle he didn't need her any more, just sleep at her side, but she had never really reached that stage. Sending her to Dublin to learn English had been the response of her parents to her lassitude, her untidiness, her neglect of her studies, her failed Bac, but they didn't know Dublin. Their friends had told them how safe, how friendly, how stimulating Dublin was. Monique would be safe in Dublin with the nice young family somebody had found for her. But they hadn't been nice. They had tried to work her like a nineteenth-century kitchenmaid and finally they had handed her over like an unwanted parcel to nice Alison and Colm.

Nice, nice, Monique kept time to the strange word every-body used as she walked along the west pier into the sunset. First useful word she had learned. Gentille, thank you, it's nice. Ça va. The police interrogations had not been nice. She hadn't understood most of the questions but Alison had helped her. The man had been found and identified and was awaiting trial, but she knew who he was anyhow, the friend of the one to whom she owed money. She wasn't afraid now. She didn't need money like that any more to hand over to the frightening people who had hounded her. Fini. And if Philippe phoned tomorrow from Paris (quel idée!) she would ask Alison or Colm to say she was not at home. Staying safely with them was better than watching the last agonies of her parents' marriage, it was preferable to looking ever again into Philippe's white face. We who are about to die salute you. Wasn't that what the doomed gladiators would say to the emperors? Tonight Monique felt so detached from it all, so indifferent to his probable death that she thought this must be happiness. The air was fresh on her skin and the lighthouse sent its blinking sword of light across the still surface of the harbour. The water was inky blue now and oily from the diesel spillage. Black masts and butterfly sails sent their reflections trembling across the tide. She would walk to the lighthouse with the last of the doggy people and then she would climb the steps and go back, not along the upper wall but over the rocks on the far side of the lower wall. She knew this walk well having often done it with Alison in the early days after her arrival. Who knows, Nathalie might have arrived at the end of the pier by now and they could have coffee together up at the hotel.

A small handful of young people had congregated below the lighthouse on the far side. She saw the glow of their cigarettes and heard their laughter before she saw them. A few lovers pursued their own business at the edges of the rock on which the lighthouse had been built. A few fishermen were casting lines into the much choppier swell on this side. As Monique passed the young people she felt fear momentarily when the catcalls started, but it was clear this was the merest salutation and no threat. Now and again since that incredible night in the house she had been terrified by the sight of a strange man if she was alone. But this stage had passed quickly and the most lasting effect of that extraordinary violation was the belief that having lived through its brief brutality she could cope with anxiety that had driven her back to heroin before. Nothing, she assured herself, can ever be so bad again. Nothing. One can live after all, learn to speak English properly and make a living here or somewhere else. She felt a little like a tradesman (and was amused by the thought) who is almost qualified but must equip himself with the right tools before claiming the right to work and live by it like everybody else.

The difference between the slapping tide on this side, which faced the open channel, and the glassy-still harbour on the other was striking and she liked it. Splintered light from the hotels along the promenade made a golden halo on the choppy surface and was lost in a smother of white foam directly below her. There were no fishermen here as she stepped from rock to rock just below the wall and very few strollers were now going by above her. All were heading in the same direction, away from the lighthouse and back to the town. One figure however appeared with the darkening sky behind him leaning over the wall, a large parcel so far as she could see held in his arms. Now and again as she picked her way along she glanced with some unease at the way the slapping waves sent widening wheels of foam almost within reach of her feet, but she was more than half-way along now to where the first break in the wall would let her up out of harm's way. She had forgotten the man with his big parcel until suddenly her vision was blotted out by a heavy falling object that (it seemed) couldn't miss her but did. It crashed with a crack of thunder practically within reach of her toes and the force of it knocked her over into another curving wheel of white foam as the huge rock went roaring down into the tide. She was shocked and trembling at the knees but unhurt as somebody came running to her rescue through the opening in the wall a few yards ahead, a spike-haired young man with a girl in jeans close behind him who held her until the trembling stopped. Then each of them took one of her arms and walked her back to safety, still clutching a scrap of paper that had been blown almost into her mouth from the draught of the falling rock. The young man took it from her gently and read aloud the three words scrawled on it PAY YOUR DEBTS. The girl said, 'I saw the guy getting away but we'll take her to the guards. Come on, love.' Monique was shocked and speechless in their hands and speechless still as they drove her with kindly assurances that she only half understood to the police station in Dun Laoire.

I I

After many postponements the davenport from Olivia was to be delivered on Friday when Denis had a free day, but he had to postpone his shopping expedition and wait in for it. His cats, who knew the shape of the week very well by now, stalked to and fro through the flat waiting for him to go before pursuing their own day in the shrubbery which surrounded the car park. It was sunny there and also there was plenty of cover. There were tenants they liked and allowed themselves to be stroked by and there were tenants from whom they determinedly hid. But first they had to assure themselves that Denis had gone about his proper business of fetching the Friday fish. Only then could they begin their day in peace.

Denis pottering uneasily about the apartment, understood their anxiety. He often talked to his cats and offered them explanations which they appeared to accept. But this morning they wound their feathery tails in and out through his legs and purred and then sat at the door with both pairs of golden eyes fixed expectantly on him. He explained he wasn't going yet but that shouldn't stop them. He opened the door for them and they wouldn't go, but started weaving in and out of his legs again. The ash-grey beauty gave her peculiar squeak of enquiry (what the hell is *on* today?) but refused to understand when he explained. The marmalade cat stared back trustfully at him, believing apparently that all would be well.

The trouble really was that Denis didn't believe he could

incorporate the once-cherished piece of furniture into his life again. It had hurt to part from it, since he'd known the little desk from childhood when his school reports were filed away there and the term's pocket money used to emerge from one of its secret drawers. But he had sawn the thing off like his house and his semi-wild garden and now he didn't know what part it could play in the new apartment. Perhaps he would just put a pot of begonias on it and leave it to be looked at and enjoyed, but where? It would probably be delivered in half an hour or so and he still hadn't decided.

But the half-hour became an hour and *The Irish Times* had been read from cover to cover before his bell rang and the cats flicked up on the window-ledge on full alert.

The CIE men were quite good about the small, valuable piece of furniture. They had packed the dozen drawers separately in thick canvas covers and the inside ones were safely locked. They carried the desk with great care through the narrow hall and on an impulse he took away the record-player and indicated a corner opposite the door of the living-room. They deposited it carefully, gave him the keys and civilly accepted the tip he offered them. Then he saw them to his apartment door and when he returned the cats were in possession, sniffing and pacing across the top with its thinning but beautifully polished green leather. Olivia had clearly made a special effort at first-class presentation. When he unpacked the drawers their brass handles were gleaming, their walnut faces glowing with new wax. The golden eyes watched him until the last drawer was in place, then they came to a unanimous decision that enough of their day had been wasted. Suddenly they jumped down and demanded to be let out and he knew they would watch for him in the shrubbery and emerge to see him off on his shopping trip.

Meanwhile he lifted the heavy sloping top of the little desk and saw that it sat as sweetly as ever on its brass hinges. The maze of little drawers fascinated him nearly as much now as when he was a child and he opened each carefully, enjoying the silky movement a long-dead cabinet maker had given it by dovetailing. The fifth drawer he opened was not quite empty and he wondered if Olivia had been able to resist putting a letter into it. There was a letter in it but it hadn't been written this morning and it hadn't been written by Olivia. He lifted out the worn, faintly familiar pale blue notepaper which was still in its original creases but which hardly made a rustle as he opened it.

> 124 Dartry Road,
> Rathmines, Dublin
> May 5th 1953.

My dear Olivia,

Your letter has made me very happy because I'd hardly dared to hope you might have enjoyed our little evening so much. *Bohème* may not be one of the great operatic master-pieces but it has always been one of my favourites and I'm delighted the humming chorus appeals to you as much as it does to me. Pure magic in last Monday's performance and enhanced that little bit more by your company at my side. It was kindness itself on your part to accept my invitation. Thank you.

Your response makes me less diffident now about suggesting a little trip for next Sunday since the weather is so lovely. Would you think of taking a tram with me to Howth and then that other little open-topped tram up on the Head where we could walk around by Bailey to Red Rock perhaps? Then if you are not in a hurry we might go further and have tea at the hotel in Sutton. Let me know what you think before Saturday my dear Olivia.

> Ever yours in hope,
> Denis

He refolded the worn letter (read many times perhaps?) and

with a shaking hand put it back in the drawer. That walk through the hot afternoon with all the long summer opening up like the gorse blossoms ahead of them had ended in the most important impulse of his life. She had received his proposal of marriage with bent head, the fingers of one hand curling and uncurling around a pebble whereas he had half-expected her to recoil. She flung back the warm bright hair into his face and laughed frankly up at him, said she thought he'd never ask her. Yes. Of course. Yes. If he really wanted to know she'd decided all of six months ago to marry him and his astonishment made him flop weakly down onto the heather where she followed and lay still laughing in his arms. Decorous days. A clasped hand had been the height of excitement for all those months and a few long kisses that afternoon with sun and sea and skylarks all around them was obviously her seal on a promise. Girls those days expected and got a slow courtship. Olivia's frankness touched and astonished him. How strange that that was the letter which she had somehow missed when clearing out the drawer. Was it the only one? He searched with his hand and found nothing but a length of blue satin ribbon. Had she kept a bundle of his letters and had that one fallen out unnoticed? Most probably. It was touching and disturbing. It was as if he had casually looked out of a window and seen himself twenty-eight years old again, and Olivia a wilful blonde twenty-two-year-old just having finished her arts course.

All day the cobwebby blue letter in the davenport stayed with him, an enchantment and a worry. What should he do with it? Put it in an envelope addressed to Olivia without comment? Ring her up and say 'I've just found the strangest thing, a ghost of thirty years ago'? Do nothing? Leave it where she had forgotten it, pushed to the back of the drawer? He found himself smiling now and again in the course of his shopping at the thought of it, but it was early evening when eventually he tried to phone Olivia, and by then she had obviously gone out. He heard the phone ring on through the empty flat and he paced his own afterwards in some unease. He would have preferred to get the thanks over and done with before Anita arrived. When she did, he found himself a little unfit for the exuberance of her. He would actually have preferred to potter about, to decide what papers and documents should go into the desk and what he should do with the freed space in the drawer below his bookshelves. He could have passed the evening very happily that way with his cats, his operatic records and his own company. But it was Friday, the cats knew it and were now pacing restlessly again. He decided to have his bath before feeding them and putting them away. Their fish poached in milk was already cooling in the saucepan. The smell was adding to their restlessness. Their soft angora fur seemed to be standing each hair on end. When you stroked them electricity tingled through your fingers.

He was calmer when he emerged from his steamy bathroom, found clean towels and put them in place, her favourite brown one for Anita, a green one for him. Then he laid as usual a soft old towel ready on the end of his bed. He was fussy about unnecessarily stained sheets and he had, of course, changed the bed that morning. The secure sense of excitement of other Fridays was missing. He felt a bit of an old fool. He even felt that Anita might have regarded him as such right from the beginning. He put his resigned cats away in the brush cupboard with greater regret than ever after their supper. And as he set the table in the fireless living-room (it was too warm for a fire these nights) he waited uneasily for the ring at the door. He waited a long time, the length of a Haydn quartet (both sides). His hands were trembling when he eventually opened the door and found Anita full of apologies and affection in equal measure. When she swung from his neck she almost unsteadied him, and when she danced him into the living-room he asked for mercy.

'I love you,' she said, wrapping him closely and fitting

herself into position to feel his response. It didn't come and tonight he knew it wouldn't. 'I love you. I love you. Don't you care, Honey Bear?'

'What do you think?' he said wanly, and she answered him at once.

'I think you are sad and out of sorts and in need of comfort tonight. I won't love you to death although I'd like to. I've just discovered something strange and wonderful, Honey Bear. I've discovered I love you better than somebody half your age that I thought I fancied. He's nice and he's even a little bit like you but it's not the same. I love you. Are you listening to me?'

'I could be your father, Anita,' he said tiredly. 'Aren't we both being a little bit silly?'

'Never! You just aren't as keen on me yet as I am on you but give it time Denis. Look at me. Would I lie to you? Let's go to bed now and eat later. Come, Honey Bear.'

'Please.' He held both her hands to keep them away from him and then politely kissed the tips of her fingers.

'OK.' She smiled in tolerant acceptance. 'What are we going to eat tonight?'

'You'll see,' he said thankfully. 'Sit down, love.'

'I'll have the candles lit by the time you get back,' she said, rummaging for matches in the accustomed place. He had forgotten to replace the empty box when shopping today but she wasn't to be thwarted. She went searching successfully around the room and when he came back he found the candles lit and Anita on her knees in rapture before the davenport. She said she had been too busy looking at him to see it earlier on. What a miracle of a lovely thing – where had he found it?

Over dinner, Denis poured the chilled white wine and didn't mince his words.

'My wife sent it to me for my birthday,' he said deliberately and watched her face. She looked unconcerned.

'Then she's very fond of you still and why not? She has excellent taste, I can tell you that.'

'It's not quite what you think,' he said unhappily. 'You see —'

Anita listened with interest to the story and nodded her head. 'She was mean about it and then regretted it on your birthday. Show's she's OK. But there *is* another explanation, Denis.' She looked at him teasingly over the candles. 'She's sorry she broke it up, Honey Bear, and I wouldn't blame her for that either. She's trying to get you back.'

'What nonsense!' he said so sharply that Anita instantly regretted she had let go what was running through her mind.

'Maybe I'm writing novels,' she said. 'Don't pay any attention to me, love. I've always had this vivid imagination. Of course she isn't trying to get you back. Who'd want to get you back once they were safely rid of you? Your little shop has never done better than this cannelloni, by the way. It's great.'

He couldn't recall any other evening when he hadn't been able to talk to her. There she was glimmering at him across the table with her newly washed hair, her eyes fixed joyfully on him, twenty-two years old and crackling with life, and he had no more interest in her body than if she were an aged grandmother. Worse, he couldn't even talk to her. He knew from her expression that he was missing half of what she was telling him about Ben's school and making all the wrong responses when he did manage to utter a sentence, but not even the wine helped and he looked into what was left of the evening with profound gloom. It was as if a wall of pebbled glass had appeared between him and Anita and he actually welcomed the phone bell when it began ringing stridently. That was another thing he missed. His own mellow-sounding bell on the old phone.

Any other Friday evening, if he had lifted the phone to hear Olivia's voice he would have been alarmed and annoyed. This evening he didn't particularly mind, although it obviously could have been better if she had been at home when he telephoned earlier. Her voice was warm and pleased and clearly she was living in the afterglow of a good deed.

'No,' he answered, 'no scratches or chips or anything. None – they were decent men and very careful. Sorry, I missed that. No, no you haven't interrupted a solitary dinner. Not at all.' The ambiguity of this pleased him. 'I did try to phone you, naturally, and you were not at home. Yes indeed. Friday is that sort of day. Yes of course I remember. Nineteen-sixty-nine it must have been. Quite so. Delightful evening. No I don't think so, but thanks for the suggestion just the same. In fact I won't be at home later. Some other time perhaps. No I haven't quite decided what specifically to use it for yet. I agree. There's a glorious amount of space. Yes you're right. I do still tend to hoard everything of that nature. The magpie instinct. It will be most useful. I could of course have done perfectly well without it. You know I meant it when I said that. Of course. No I haven't really examined it too closely yet. [Liar!] Of course. Good night. And thank you again.'

When he put the phone down his face was flushed like a young man's from lying and he went back awkwardly to the table where Anita was waiting. She had put both plates back into the oven again and came with him into the kitchen to get them. But from her kneeling position at the oven she suddenly twisted back and embraced his thighs so gently at such a remembered childish angle that his resistance half melted and when she slid her arms up around his neck as she got to her feet and kissed him with all the frankness he had been trying to evade, he resisted no longer and went with her when she whispered, 'Let's eat later, hm?' In bed, however, he failed her for the first time in almost a year and was deeply ashamed.

'It happens, Honey Bear,' she said kindly. 'It's not the end of the world, you know. You're tired and upset and the phone call was the last straw. Who cares?'

He was surprised at the variety of caresses she lavished on

him that were hardly sexual at all and he was surprised, too, to wake up tumescent and alone in the first daylight. He found a little note from her on the table saying she had eaten up her supper before going home and she hoped to see him even before next Friday if he would like to telephone.

12

The letter was put into Ben's hands as he left for work. It had been re-addressed by his mother and it was a little crumpled by two journeys through the post. Mr Coyle was anxious to claim some credit for having intercepted the postman again when he was about to take the letter away.

'Mighta thrun it in the Liffey,' said Mr Coyle, 'nor it wouldn't be first time neither. Can't get it into their heads there's people living in this house again, not just yours truly. Glad I caught the bugger in the nick of time, son.'

'Thank you, Mr Coyle. This is a letter I'd be sorry not to have got.'

In truth it was. It made a warm lining to his pocket as he walked through the summer morning to school. Nobody could mistake the elegant back-sloping hand, the lack of punctuation throughout the address. He imagined the remembered chewed top of her pen, the bitten nails which bunched around it. He saved the opening of it for his break, and as he read and re-read, the coffee cooled and died in his cup. As usual she addressed him as though they had seen one another yesterday.

Ben, I don't think so. One day I dropped in to see the parents and your letter was there. Two months old letter? You said yours was like putting a message in a bottle and throwing it into the tide so I suppose this is too. In two months you could have gone away again or moved out of home and your mother probably will have done what mine did. 'If I leave this in the hall she'll come sometime.' So she did. So you will maybe. I don't see the point of meeting again Ben. You can't help nor can anybody now and anyhow it doesn't matter. I live with a few people who can give me all I need which is sleep. But if I ever meet you anywhere by chance you will tell me maybe about Ingeborg Schnell.

Be happy
Julie.

No address. No phone number. She was probably living with a coven of junkies and she was probably right that he couldn't help her any more. A burnt-out case at twenty-six? A statistic? But he knew he couldn't leave it like that. In the classroom with its shouting hordes, at break outside, he knew he would somehow find a way to see her. Right away he phoned Anita and asked her where she would look in Dun Laoire if she wanted to buy hard drugs. She suggested that he drop in during the week to her office and she would give him a list of places. A very long list, she stressed.

He saw what she meant when he eventually did drop in to see her. She had typed out two pages for him and he took them gratefully, doubly grateful because she bore no grudge apparently for his unwillingness to pursue something accidentally begun. He invited her to lunch with him that day and she accepted it with detached friendliness. Over the coffee she smiled levelly across at him.

'I take it you're looking for somebody rather than going to market,' she said, and (not seeing any reason for concealment) he nodded and mentioned Julie's name. She brought her brows together and rummaged in a small notebook out of her bag.

'It's a long shot,' she said, 'but I never forget a name and she has a particular health problem if I'm thinking of the same girl – maybe not. Try these two addresses.' She wrote quickly and firmly, tore the page out of her notebook and gave it to him. He covered her hand and squeezed it before taking the paper and she blinked before smiling.

'We'll always be friends but you're not worthy of me, are you? I have the strangest feeling that if I'm not very lucky your father will say the same.'

'No he won't,' Ben said quickly. 'Look, it's difficult to put words on. You know that.'

'But,' she interrupted confidently.

'But it's one hell of a strange situation and I don't know how to handle it, except by running away. For I think the first time in my life I'm embarrassed and very guilty about creating a scenario in which we both probably acted a bit out of character.'

'I didn't and we both created the scenario, if that's what it was. I work with so much misery every day of my life that I never look a gift horse in the mouth if I like him and feel comfortable with him. This is 1984 and it just may be the end of the line. For all of us.'

'I won't pursue that well-worn argument. But what I meant to say is, my father's at the time of his life when a rare piece of good fortune like you, Anita, is the exception and not the rule.'

'I'm not too sure about that,' Anita said at last. 'But I love the guy. I'd settle down with him tomorrow if he gave me so much as a hint that he'd like it. What appealed to me powerfully about you is that you're very like him.'

'I deserved that,' Ben grinned. He felt happier than he'd felt since it happened. It was OK. There were not going to be any problems. And if there were, they would not be in relation to Anita and him.

He left the restaurant full of gratitude for her pragmatic good sense and kindness. Those pages from her notebook might lead him yet to the right place.

At the end of the first Saturday's search he felt depressed. He had left the work on the swimming pool in the hands of a few fellows he had come to rely on and he had crossed the city instead to his parents' side of the river and beyond it to the seaside town which had as bad a drug problem as the inner city. It was a sharp bright day in early summer, more like a spring day because of the breeze, but the first tourists of the season had already arrived. His instinct on such a day would be to stay out of doors until the light was gone but you didn't ever search out of doors for Julie. Even without Anita's list, he would have looked in pubs or dim cafés or in basement rooms. Julie didn't like the sun which tended to hurt her eyes and burn her skin at a touch. He sat around watching, pretending to read a newspaper in light that was too dim, and he saw the deals being made, the gear being exchanged, the largely silent battles for dominance. He knew that although he might find Julie in such places, he would never find the protected businessmen who made all the money. The little people he was watching were addicts themselves, smalltime dealers who'd buy two grams of heroin perhaps at £250, cut and distribute them and make £300, or use the lot and owe the money to people who would not stop short of violence. In a haze of smoke and dim light Ben watched and waited but came home eventually with a headache and a deep sense of futility. Once in Zurich on a hot day in July he had seen upwards of a hundred junkies scattered throughout a public park near Beustweg along the lakeside. Male and female, they lay prone on the grass among the azaleas, many of them with heavily bandaged arms or ulcerated legs covered in surgical gauze. The sun was shining, they were younger than he was and they might have been dead. They were never hungry, they were never horney, they were never curious, they were never thinking of anything but the next fix. He watched the painful awakening of one young girl with a grey face and thin flaky brown hair. She averted her eyes from the sun, shivered, lifted one huge bandaged leg into a more comfortable position with both hands, and then curled over into a foetal position before closing her eyes again. Somebody he met in a bar told him the police liked to keep moving the junkies around from district to district. This was their current centre, and later in a men's lavatory he heard the sounds of a man and a woman in the same cubicle trying with difficulty to inject one another into collapsed veins. The crying of the woman stayed in his ears for a long time and he remembered it when he reached home that Saturday night.

Why bother about Julie? She might be all right. She had indeed kicked the habit on several occasions and grown almost healthy again, or as healthy as she would ever be. She had tried to explain to him once that she liked the small enclosed world of the druggies, their feeling for one another, their sense of exclusion from banalities that were everybody else's lot, the endless absorption with how the market was going, prices, sources, dealers, quality, the whole folklore of the drug user, the indifference to death. He knew it was just possible that he would never get through to her again any more than he could hold a conversation with a fish at the bottom of a pool, but he became obsessed with the effort, convinced especially on the next Saturday that he would walk in somewhere and find her. He even went to the launderette where he had stumbled on her the first time, but she was not there and, in the end, to his total astonishment she phoned him one day at school and asked if they could meet. He had a sense of complete unreality as he waited for her in the same city bar where he had been offered the smuggling job on his first day home. Julie had liked this place in the old days and she evidently liked it still. He watched her before she saw him, moving quickly in a long-sleeved white dress among the beautiful people. Her hair was shining and flowing free and she was smiling even before she saw him. He felt extraordinarily happy at the sight of her, remembering the sort of places where he had searched for her.

'Hello Ben?

'Julie.'

They kissed and then impulsively he bent and kissed her again on the eyelids, since she reached only to his chin.

'You can't ever imagine how glad I am to see you. I've been searching here and there off and on for you. You're well – I can see it. Well and beautiful again.'

'Tolerably.' This was as much as she would ever concede and he laughed at her, happy for the first time in weeks. She might have been a different human being from the wrecked girl in the launderette, but then Julie had always changed from hour to hour.

'Before we forget, tell me at once about Ingeborg Schnell,' said Julie.

'There's nothing more to tell than I put in the letter. I said I'd show you. Here.' He had taken care to put the small wrapped parcel in an inner pocket and he handed it over to her now with a feeling of keen pleasure. She opened it as eagerly almost as his niece had done and she stared with no less delight into the world inside a matchbox that Ingeborg Schnell had made, the enamel stove and the black cat, the copper pots and pans, the trailing plants hanging from the square window with its square piece of lace hung on hooks, the blue and white apron of the microscopic figure stirring something in a wooden bowl. This was not the same as the matchbox he had given to young Olivia. Ingeborg Schnell never exactly repeated her effects.

'Dutch Interior,' Julie said. 'I don't believe the miracle of it.' She touched the copper pan with a fingernail and laughed softly.

'Look,' Ben said. 'Open the cupboard door.' She did and inside were jars of oil and cheese, jampots and spice jars, all the right size for a mosquito to handle.

'Who was this Ingeborg Schnell? I love her,' Julie said, giggling as he had not heard her giggle for years.

'I told you,' said Ben, but he told her again about the sad junkie from Düsseldorf who made these little masterpieces to help feed her habit.

'Thank you for such a magic thing, Ben,' she said at last, closing the box and putting it away in a draw-string leather bag. 'But you're making the old mistakes all over again. She's maybe a very happy junkie like me, unwilling to be reformed and cleaned up like everybody else.'

'She has no wish one way or the other about it now,' Ben said. 'She's dead.'

'Careless of her, or else it was what she wanted,' Julie said lightly. 'I'm so happy to see you again, Ben. I phoned your mother at last and she told me where you were.'

'You look wonderful,' he said again. 'It makes me very happy to see you too.'

'It's because I've come to a decision, you see. I'm going away again.'

His heart gave a painful jump. 'Why?'

'Because this is a dead city and I should have realised it before. Guilt-ridden, hopeless and dead, and I've had enough. I'm going to Haarlem, to catalogue a library. It's only about forty miles from Amsterdam.'

'Alone?'

'Of course alone.' She laughed again. 'I can't wait to be gone, but first I had to see you. Poor worrying Ben. If I could stay with anybody for ever it would be with you!'

'But your letter?' he said. 'It wasn't cheerful. You said all you needed was sleep.'

'Doesn't everybody? But I don't need it all the time, Ben. I was ill when I wrote that letter. I'm very well now.'

'Clean?'

'Mind your own business, Ben. We never did agree on how life is best conducted for people like me. I'm happy. I have a job waiting for me. It's OK. Trust me.'

'With anything but your own best interest,' he said, gloomily, and then he changed tack. Why not take this meeting for what it was, a fond leavetaking? 'Forgive me, Julie. Tell me again what you're going to do, so that I can imagine you

130

among the tulips and the lotus-eaters. Whose *is* this library?'

She began to talk. The library belonged to a business associate of her father's, and it was inherited from *his* father. It contained, among other things, art books of considerable importance and some of Europe's earliest printed books. It had never been properly catalogued and this Mr Tappe wanted somebody to live in and see what could be done in a year. The money would be very good.

'Maybe you'll come and see me, Ben?'

'Maybe I will. I remember spending one chilly summer's afternoon in Haarlem and it was beautiful. Little cobbled lanes and courtyards full of cats. The Franz Hals Museum. A lovely canal walk.'

'All that,' said Julie happily, 'and friends in Amsterdam whenever I want to go up, and friends in Lieden too.'

'Have you met this Mr Tappe?'

'Only once, but he's OK. My father has stayed at his house and he has a wife who is a doctor and servants, would you believe it? There's no question of slaving away as an au pair or anything like that. I'll just work in the library and make my own hours.'

'You even have me envious, Julie.'

'I'll write and let you know whether or not you need to be.'

'Promise?'

'Promise!'

He looked delightedly down at her happy face and realised the only visible difference between her and the beautiful creatures all around her was that they were brown and she was pale. They wore dresses with clipped sleeves or none and she was buttoned like a nun into her cuffed dress. She wanted (to his great surprise) to see St Domenic's, so they crossed the city hand in hand, walking as she suggested. That was another improvement. Julie had usually hated to walk anywhere but now she kept pace with him in her black buttoned boots – he suddenly noticed that the boots would not have looked out of place on a late nineteenth-century lady going bicycling.

'Do you remember when your mother came visiting us in Germany,' she asked him suddenly, 'and I was so petrified I got into the linen box?'

'Could I forget it? I expected to find you smothered when I eventually got back. I was anxious as hell.'

'Ben the Worrier,' she said, smiling affectionately up at him with that face of the girl who had always been afraid of everything but who (perhaps) had grown up at last.

'If you would only promise me before you go to throw away that crutch you think you need. I know how to get you first-class professional advice and treatment and you could be free of hard drugs for ever. When are you going away?'

'Next month, and after all, *you* haven't changed have you? I am in control now better than I've ever been in my whole life. I'm in no danger – or in considerably less than if the doctors started fucking up my mind with something else, as they did before and would do again if I let them. I'm an inadequate personality, as they call it, who has worked out for *herself* how to stay alive with the minimum help. Now can we leave it if you don't mind?'

'OK. I almost do believe you.'

She smiled and shrugged off her annoyance and walked wonderingly with him through the unlovely surroundings he had chosen for his own. They got curious stares, catcalls and friendly greetings in about equal proportion from the pupils who always hung around the school on Saturdays since he had pleaded to have the playground left open, some half-heartedly working on the swimming pool, some playing pitch and toss, some reading comics in sheltered corners and some hanging around talking, smoking and scuffling with one another. At times like these, when he came upon them unexpectedly congregated in the only place where the less troubled of them seemed to feel at home he felt a kinship with them which made him understand why he had almost decided to stay on after the summer holidays.

'Suppose,' Julie said, thought-reading as she had always done, 'suppose I tried to find you a job in Haarlem, what then?'

'Tell me when you do, and then we'll see,' he said, leaving it on her own playful level. He had been down that road before and he had to be cautious this time. But suddenly it felt like all the young summers he had ever known, the time for dreams of liberation, even of happy-ever-afters. Smiling at the friendly catcalls all around him, he led her to his crumbling house, the small remembered hand with the bitten-down nails still tightly held in his own.

13

Stephen Lydon read the letter with the government stamp on it, and he knew he was not dreaming after all. He was to get enough help from the organisers of a Youth Training programme to finish the swimming pool before the end of term. He had decided to apply to them for permission to keep it open with an appointed caretaker for the long summer holidays. What use to the area was a swimming pool that would close in June and not re-open until September? There was a month now to get the building finished and the pool operational and he would think about finding a caretaker when he knew he wasn't fooling himself. He lifted the phone to accept the offer formally and smiled as the voice asked him to follow the call with a letter of verification. He said he would do that and then he made another phone call with the smile still on his face. He listened this time to the ringing of the phone with real pleasure, following the sound in his mind through the elegant apartment and seeing Olivia walk to the receiver.

'Hello my dear. I think I'd like to tell you at once that we've got the help we need for the pool largely through an intelligent hunch Ben had which worked.'

'I'm so glad for you.' And she sounded it too.

'And', he went on smiling as if she were there, 'I want to tell you too that inviting me home that evening was the luckiest thing that's happened to me for years. You *and* Ben have turned a hopeless situation into a cakewalk. I'm truly grateful.

But why don't you let me tell you all the details over lunch in Hunter's tomorrow? It's perfect weather for it.'

'Perfect. There's nothing I'd like better than a trip into the country. Thank you, I'll come.'

'Pick you up tomorrow at twelve noon!'

'See you then, Stephen.'

He had always liked her voice from the first moment she leaned over in a restaurant and asked if she might borrow his newspaper to check the starting time of a film. He had been about to go to that same film himself, but had thought it would be too corny a move to say so. However, when it was over and they were both emerging out of the darkness he had greeted her and invited her to have a coffee with him. Smiling she had examined him and hesitated a long time before saying yes. But having said it, she had charmed him by behaving as though they had known one another all their lives. They had met briefly for a drink and to go to an exhibition every two weeks or so. After that came the evening when she asked him home to dinner. That had been a watershed for him and he felt he had been given permission to take it from there. She was naturally more interested than ever in the school since Ben had come to work there. He had given her flowers recently, which she hadn't rejected. He might bring a single red rose to lunch with him tomorrow.

The ways of courtship were half-forgotten. He knew he was inclined to move either too fast or too slowly. His timing, he knew, had never been quite right and maybe his marriage had suffered from that. But increasingly now he had begun to feel quite easy with Olivia. She was calm. She didn't take fright easily or ever try to rush him. She was a worldly and confident lady and he had grown tired of picking up broken pieces, tired of new beginnings which led down a very old road. Olivia had been and was like a breath of fresh air. She didn't have to be cosseted or have her confidence boosted. She met him on equal terms and if he lost her (although he thought it unlikely) it would be in fair open contest. He thought she would be the perfect mate for a schoolmaster, kind and decisive, fond of young people and able to handle them. Look at the job she had made of Ben! Of her husband he didn't need to think. That was her own business. She would not have broken that up without good and logical reason. One didn't have to think for Olivia. That was the most restful thing about her. And he didn't think one would have to pretend any passionate love for her either. That might come later after they had been sleeping together for a while if they were lucky. Now it was enough to enjoy her company, to look forward to the look on her face when they met again and the friendly warmth of her voice. Nothing need be prejudged or taken for granted. He wasn't dealing with an unsure girl.

So his spirits rose as he drove south to the coast to pick her up. She was the exact antithesis of his work at school, of all that deviousness which was necessary if young things already threatened were not either to be crushed or given less support than they needed. His passion was the school. He thought Olivia would understand that all he could offer at the moment was hope and a strong inclination to become involved in everything that concerned her. And a red rose. She took it gracefully, then laughed and shook her head at him. On the way down to Ashford through the greening countryside she broke off at times to exclaim over some effect of light or shade but always returned to the problems of St Domenic's. Her interest did not seem to be merely polite but genuine because the school concerned her son and himself so closely. He found himself telling her about the return to school this week at her own request of Pauline Devlin, the child involved in the incest case.

'Yes,' she said, 'Ben filled me in on that horror story. The poor helpless child. How is she?'

'Much better than anybody would have believed possible,' he said. 'Playing football again and in the good care of foster parents. Ben is insisting on giving her extra lessons in his own spare time so that she can catch up again. She's a great kid, a fighter and I think a winner.'

'The dice are so unfairly loaded against some children,' Olivia said with a catch in her voice. 'I'm not surprised to hear Ben has stepped in. As a little boy he was always helping lame dogs over stiles but he'd never leave it at that. Bring them home with him – nine cases out of ten.'

'And what would you do?'

'Bandage them, butter them with kind words, feed them, and cast them out. I'm a realist you see.' She unwrapped the red rose, broke two-thirds off the stem and stuck the flower in the buttonhole of her cream jacket.

They were sitting down to lunch at the same time as Ben was meeting Julie and they were returning from a walk in the state forest when Pauline Devlin, who had been let in by Mr Coyle, tapped gently on the door of Ben's flat. She had to knock louder before the door was opened and then she was made shy by the presence of a strange young woman who in fact said she was just going.

'I'll give you a ring before I go, Ben,' she said, amid Pauline's protests that she would come back tomorrow. Then Pauline turned away while they kissed, and the young woman ran off down the stairs, and the schoolmaster said, 'Wait for me in there, Pauline – I've forgotten something,' and he was off down the rickety stairs after his friend.

'I'm sorry, sir,' she said, when he came back. 'I cudda kem tomorrow or any day. It wouldn't matter, sir!'

'Sit down there and stop blathering, Pauline. You're welcome. Don't forget you came by arrangement. Read through this page down to the second last paragraph while I get my notes in the next room. I can't remember where I decided to start with you.'

She was sitting with bent head when he came back, the book still open in her hands.

137

'Tell me what you think of that conversation between Janey, Mary and her mother. Would she talk like that do you think?'

The spikey black hair sank lower still and when Ben took the book of short stories from her hand he saw that she was crying. It took him only a moment to understand why.

'You can't read very well yet, Pauline, isn't that it?' The spikey head nodded and lifted a bit before she spoke in such a low voice that he had to bend to hear it.

'I – I never seemed to catch on to reading like the others, Mr Ryan. I don't seem to be able to make sense of the letters – but I know them, like . . .' she added desperately.

'Of course you do, so it's not going to take you long to read. I know what we'll do. We'll begin with a newspaper – today's *Evening Press*. See that story? Well, I'm going to copy out the first two sentences in big letters here. Look Pauline:

A MAN IN HIS SIXTIES WAS KNOCKED DOWN BY A PASSING CAR AS HE CROSSED BAGGOT STREET BRIDGE LATE LAST NIGHT. THE DRIVER DID NOT STOP.

'Now you know A? What's M–A–N? What does it sound like?'

She was in fact extraordinarily quick and he formed his plan for her that afternoon. A week only with a part-time literacy expert whom he knew quite well and then he would take her over himself for the rest of the term. How would that suit her?

'Would the mates in class know, sir?'

'How would they, unless you tell them? This friend of mine lives over in Dorset Street. You'd have to go there three evenings next week if he can take you. I think he'd do it if I asked him – he's the best man I know for getting people quickly through the early stages. He has a new technique with a tape-recorder, invented by himself. OK, Pauline?'

'OK, sir.' Her eyes were dry and she was grinning at him now.

'No, don't go yet, Pauline. We'll do a page of this story "Araby" because it may be the first good story you will read for yourself. It's all about this crush a young fellow has on a young girl who lives nearby – he hardly knows her at all.'

As Ben spoke he realised how remote Pauline Devlin would be from the processes of adolescent courtship. She looked like any other girl from these parts, but it was in the very nature of her traumatic experience that she would know nothing about how ordinary young people went about the business of wooing. The crazed brutality of her encounters with her father and her brothers seemed on the surface, however, to have left little trace. He supposed the psychiatrists had brought her to terms with the untimely start of her adult life as efficiently as the doctors had rid her of disease, but nobody could totally undo what had been done to her. All he could contribute was literacy which might (if the inclination was there) liberate her mind into the saner world of literature. She was fourteen. *Jane Eyre* might mean something to her soon. *Great Expectations*. The novels about adolescence of Alan Garner. Untrained as he was in psychology he felt that what a child like this one needed was to find her way back to the real world through books, and he thought he could help her with a carefully selected programme. The other way he could perhaps help her was by encouraging her to talk about herself.

'Tell me,' he made the beginning as a break in the work, 'tell me, Pauline, about your new family. Do you like them?'

'They're all right,' the girl said. 'The mother is nice and kind and she can make good nosh and he's not bad. Gives you a few orders, but friendly like!'

'What about the children?'

'I like Sandra – she's my age – and I don't like Paul or Tony, but Paschal the baby is dishy. Paul and Tony are all right but you can't bear to have them shouting into your ear all the time.'

'But they'll grow up and get sense.'

'Yeh,' Pauline said, without enthusiasm. She was, he concluded happily, quite like an elder sister being mildly annoyed with her noisy brothers. Already these people seemed to be her family. But there was something which worried him about her insistence on returning to her old school.

'Do you ever see any of your own family around here now?'

It was very warm up here but she shivered as he spoke and averted her eyes from him.

'They're all in jail still and I hope they stay there – all except Tommy.'

'Tommy?'

'The one who's sixteen. He was all right until they made him drunk one night. He's the one who looks like Mammy.'

'All the same I think you had probably better forget him. You have a family now who love you and want to keep you for as long as you'd like to stay.'

'Yeh,' Pauline said again, and he wondered if he should have probed her at all. He went back to the newspaper paragraph again and she seemed to be reading it before he let her go. In fact he thought it was just that she had been blessed or cursed with an exceptionally good memory. She lived only a short fare away and he saw her safely onto the bus before he let himself go smiling back into thoughts of Julie again.

14

Sunday lunch in Monkstown was at times a fairly elaborate affair, when Olivia took pleasure in remembering she had a family again. She would make elaborate preparations on Saturday and be certain to have the sort of dishes that could be cooked in advance and put into the oven to be ready in half an hour. Starters and desserts went into the fridge, already prepared in little dishes, and Ben would always do a large green salad for her. Sometimes on Sunday it was only the two of them and anyhow he always came first and they talked while setting the table.

The Sunday following her lunch in the country with Stephen Lydon was one of those days when she was entertaining Alison and Colm too so she was particularly glad to see Ben arriving early with his two bottles of white wine and a big smile. She noted his relaxed air and the way he beamed at her, obviously glad to be here. He noticed her agitation and the way she kept taking things up and putting them down again in the same place.

'Have a sherry with me, Ben, because I want your advice?'

'Glad to.' He noticed she still favoured his father's favourite San Patricio and he felt a sudden hostility in himself when she sat him down at the window facing the sea and leaned with her back to the table beside him.

'I could beat about the bush with you, Ben, but I won't. Stephen has asked me to live with him and I don't know what to do. You know both of us – advise me.'

Ben put down his head and laughed into his sherry. She really was an original. There she was looking down at him with an imploring look on her face as though their roles were reversed.

'I don't see how I can *possibly* advise you any further than to say please yourself – nobody else is involved except Stephen and he has asked you.'

'You're not *trying* to understand, Ben. You know I'm – I'm fond of your father still and this would be so definitive – going to live with another man or having him live here as *of course* it would have to be. Environment is so important to me and I've put a lot into this place. I think on the whole he'd be perfectly willing to share it, but that's not the point.'

'What is the point, Mother?'

She sighed, closed her eyes briefly as though in pain and shook her head at him. 'How can you ask, Ben? Your father is the point, now and always and forever.'

'But you walked out on him. Made him sell his house – and yours – and scatter everything you'd built up together over a lifetime. Was that not definitive enough?'

'Don't you dare judge me, Ben. You couldn't possibly understand what it's like to be a woman and *submerged* in the life of your family. Life should be a cycle. We had come to the end of ours together when you and Alison went your own ways and I had to see if there was anything of my own I could accomplish that would have nothing to do with Denis.'

'Quite so, and you did it and you've managed beautifully, haven't you, built up all this for *yourself* and now a man you are fond of who may be in love with you – I couldn't know – wants to live with you. Where's the problem? Is this not the high point of independent living when you can voluntarily decide to share it?'

'You force me to abase myself, Ben. The point is if I do ever live with a man again I think he will be your father. *Now* do you understand?'

'You mean you intend to force him to live with you again, having walked out voluntarily on him?'

This time (and it had been only a matter of time) her pale blue eyes suddenly filled with tears and she was facing the sea light in front of the window.

'Never, Ben, never. But can I help hoping he will not be hard and unfeeling but respond to a very genuine change of heart on my part?'

'I think you'd be very foolish to have any hopes of that sort, Mother. I can't see it happening.' And yet he suddenly thought of smiling Julie the afternoon before. That had been a sort of marriage, his and hers, and she apparently had second thoughts about it now. But Ben reminded himself it was not the same. They hadn't lived most of their lives together and anyhow *he* had walked out on her. Also, Julie had hardly been serious. Yet looking now at his tearful mother, he wasn't so sure.

'Will you stay back and talk to me about it this evening? Please, Ben.'

'OK.'

'We might go for a walk around by the harbour,' she said and he saw her tears drying up like magic as the sound of Alison's car came up to them from the drive.

'Do I look OK, Ben?'

'You look fine, Mother.' He didn't know how old he had been when that question had first been thrown at him (five or six) and he turned away now to smile again.

She obviously forgot her own problem completely when she welcomed Alison and Colm and the grandchildren.

Normally Monique came to the lunch parties too and took the children for a walk afterwards, but where was Monique today? She hugged the children as Alison launched into her story, throwing off garments in all directions which Ben

143

sensibly picked up and hung in the hall. Alison seemed as agitated as her mother.

'I don't know what we'll do without Monique, Mother,' Alison was saying when he got back and at once hoisted his niece up on his shoulder. 'She was so *good* to the children even after the dreadful experience but this latest horror was the last straw. She was literally terrified, you see, and I know we shouldn't be in the least surprised that she wanted at last to go home. We left her at the airport yesterday, but she may have to come back if those hideous drug traffickers are brought to trial. The guards explained to us how difficult it is even although they are certain they *know* who tried to kill her on Dun Laoire pier. The same lot who broke into the house and raped her.'

'Alison!' Colm said warningly, and Ben hitched the small person up a bit on his shoulder and collected her woolly jacket from the hall which he had helped remove only a few minutes ago.

'Let me *down*, Ben,' she said, wriggling like an eel in his arms. He tightened his grip unfairly until he had run with her down the steps and headed for the sea. Then he set her down like a small rumpled hen.

'Where are we going, Ben?' She was now perfectly agreeable to go for this impromptu walk in the cool breeze along the sea wall. She wanted to walk on top of it and she dirtied her red gingham dress in the effort to scramble up there. He tipped her up the rest of the way and took a tight grip of her hand.

'Did you know before Alison told you that Monique has gone home to her Mammy, Ben?'

'No, I didn't.'

'She told me first,' the child said proudly.

'Will you miss her?' he asked gently.

'I do miss her now. But Monique said I can go to visit her in Paris when I am bigger. She said she will keep writing letters until Colm and Alison let me go.'

'Great. You'll like Paris.'

'Monique will take me on a boat along the river and bring me roasted chestnuts. She says Paris is lovely.'

'Yes it is. You're lucky.'

Up on the wall, she was nearer to his level and she stopped suddenly and looked with her mother's familiar brown eyes into his.

'Monique was afraid so that's why she had to go, Ben. I saw the person she was afraid of.'

'What did he look like?'

'Like a big giant with a mask. He was shouting. He locked me in the loo. When he was gone Monique let me out and she was crying. She let me into bed with her. My brother was still asleep. He never wakens up now until morning.'

'Tell me which school you will go to?'

'To play-school first. My friend Alan goes to play-school too. Alison will bring my brother into the office with her every morning because he doesn't wake up early. Then we'll all go walking to Herbert Park in the afternoon, see?'

'I see. Will you write maybe to Monique?'

'I can't write, Ben. If you hold my hand the way Daddy did for Alison's birthday card then I can write to her.'

'Here,' Ben said, 'I have had this nice postcard in my pocket for ages. Look.'

He lifted her down, then sat her up on the wall again and took out his biro.

'Here, lean on this. What do you want to write to Monique?'

'I'll write that I'll come to Paris in the summer.'

'But this is the summer. She said when you are bigger.'

'Then I'll write that I'll come next year.'

'And send her your love?'

'She knows that, Ben.'

'Here, we'll write it anyway. And you *can* sign your name by yourself – your grandmother told me that you can.'

'Of course I can.' The name which she wrote with a spidery

145

flourish would have to be taken on trust but he expected Monique would recognise it.

'I'll get the address from your mother and I'll post it for you. OK?'

'OK, Ben. Where will you get a stamp on Sunday?'

'I get a stamp in my pocket-book on Sunday. Look. Do you want to stick it on?'

'Yes. It says 29p.'

'Good girl. We'll stick it on here.'

'I will, I will.'

She got it on upside down but he didn't suppose it would matter.

'Thank you for the stamp, Ben. Now we'll go home to Gran's, won't we?'

'If you like. Dinner should be ready now anyway.'

Just before they went up the steps, Olivia plucked at his knees.

'Lift me up, Ben.' When she was on a level with his face she said, 'That man hurt Monique in our house and then he tried to hurt her again on the pier. Why, Ben?'

'Because he wanted to take all the money she had – he probably had none of his own. People who are not very good people to begin with get worse when they have no money of their own.'

'I see. Do you want to see where I've put Ingeborg Schnell's matchbox house?'

Indoors there was an air of great cheerfulness and Colm put a glass of wine into his hand.

'Thanks for that piece of quick thinking, Ben,' he said, and Ben winked at him. He liked this brother-in-law of his and couldn't quite equate him with what he knew of other fashionable people in that profession. During lunch Colm had them all weeping with laughter over his latest commission, to convert a nice plain Georgian house outside Dundalk into a rich smuggler's idea of a gentleman's residence. The man had made his money (something like half a million) by filling tankers with cheap petrol in the north and selling it south of the border at the higher rate in all of the three garages he owned.

'He wants a cocktail bar in one corner of the beautiful big drawing-room and I can't talk him out of it. He wants to convert an ancient conservatory that looks like the Crystal Palace into a sauna and I think I have just succeeded in making him retain the structure with a sauna unit inside. He wants battlements around the valley roof and a watchtower at one end. He wants to pull out the beautiful plain old entrance and fit Gothic arches and he wants an open plan that will eliminate the stone-flagged hall where there are two Adam fireplaces. He wants to convert the library into a billiard-room and he wants every bedroom to have its own bathroom. I'm trying to talk him into an attic conversion job for the bathrooms, approached by a spiral staircase which won't spoil the rooms. Something like your studio, Olivia, you know.'

'You made *such* a beautiful job of that, Colm,' Olivia said gratefully. 'I don't know that I'm worthy of it. Sometimes I think I'm wasting my time.'

'Show us what you've done since last time and we'll tell you,' Alison said cheerfully. The thing about Alison was that she never allowed herself to be submerged in her own worries for long and lunch parties (even her mother's) were sacred. Ben found himself detached somewhat by thinking about the fate of that poor sullen girl Monique with whom he had such slight acquaintance. He remembered not much more than the sound of rock music on ORTF coming down the stairs from her room and her brief response to their introduction. 'Enchanté,' with a heavy smile which was obviously difficult to achieve. Here, on the other hand, were his sister and her husband who must have been shattered by the girl's misfortunes under their roof, here they were making amusing chatter about rich men and bad taste and about Olivia's future as Grandma Moses.

147

When they all adjourned upstairs to the studio after lunch he loaded up the dishwasher with the help of the small girl and then read to her from a Beatrix Potter book his mother had brought from the old house. There they were in a special corner of her built-in bookshelves low down so that children could easily get at them. He was amused to find his own name on *The Tale of Benjamin Bunny* in unsteady block capitals: BENJAMIN D. RYAN, AGED 6 YEARS. 52 VICTORIA TERRACE, DUBLIN 6, IRELAND, THE WORLD, N. HEMISPHERE. IF THIS BOOK SHOULD CHANCE TO ROAM, BOX ITS EARS AND SEND IT HOME. He also read that to little Olivia and she rocked laughing, sitting chunky and cross-legged at his feet. She repeated the old tag correctly after him and listened with total attention to half of the misfortunes of Benjamin Bunny. When they got to the arrival of Benjamin's father who paced the top of the wall with a little switch in his hand looking for his son, she said with perfect good manners, 'Excuse me, Ben,' and went shouting up the stairs to find her parents. 'If this book should chance to roam, box its ears and send it home,' her voice came back down the stairs to him.

Ben wandered over to the basket to watch her sleeping brother, the shape of whose head reminded him of his father's. It was his father who used to read stories to him and Alison every evening in the nursery. They progressed from *Benjamin Bunny* and *Peter Rabbit* to the much longer *Pigling Bland* and then to *The Phoenix and the Carpet*, *The Wind in the Willows* and *The Borrowers*. 'The noblest scene in English literature is when Pod confronts the aggressive blackbird in defence of his family,' Denis had said. What was that from? *The Borrowers Afield* probably. And then there was *David Copperfield* and a line of other Dickens books. The readings went on long after both he and Alison could read, until secondary school almost, and then they got self-conscious about it and made excuses until their father grinned at them one teatime and said, 'Well that's a load off my back at last — away and do your own reading from this out, the pair of you.' He knew now it had made them readers for pleasure all their lives. He looked again at Olivia's little shelves of children's books, and noted that most of the inscriptions were from his father. It occurred to him for the first time that Denis was much more cut off from his own grandchildren than she was and this must be a sadness for him. He would no doubt read to young Olivia too if the opportunity arose. He would be reading to her this afternoon and if he were (Ben suddenly knew) she would listen to the end as Alison and he always had. There was something about the way he read stories to you which made you half-believe for as long as it took to tell the tale that he must be making it up as he went along. When they were very small he used to do just that, in fact, and Ben vaguely remembered *The Boy who Talked to Trees* and a long involved story about a little steam engine that left the main tracks one day and went down a forgotten siding into the place where old steam engines go. There was another story about a giant who just wanted to play with the children who were all afraid of him. Or was that Oscar Wilde perhaps? One day he would take young Olivia by herself to see her grandfather, for her own sake as much as for his. His father had never treated children patronisingly. He always spoke to them and read to them as equals.

When they all came down at last they exclaimed over the pot of tea Ben had ready for them, but in fact this kindness had only been a displacement activity for him. He was uneasy and even upset by the undertones of this luncheon party and his mother's words to him before it began. He wanted to get away from her, out for a long walk into the fresh air, but of course when eventually he was out in the smoky-rose light of the summer's evening, out beyond the Mariners' Church, it was with her, and she had something on her mind which she was clearly determined to have out with him.

Ignoring his silence, she chattered glibly on about the afternoon with Alison and Colm, how big the baby was growing, how clever her granddaughter was and how much better they would all be once the disturbance of that poor French girl was over. Alison would be much better looking after her own children as *she* had always done and Colm was a tower of strength and good sense.

'Will she discard him when the nest is bare?' Ben wondered wickedly out loud. 'When he's outlived his biological function will he be cast out to survive as best he can?'

'Stop it, Ben, I can't talk to you when you're in this bitter mood, and it's *precisely* about Denis that I wish to talk to you.'

Of course he knew this, but they had walked another mile of gathering clouds and were in fact back at her apartment again before he stopped plugging every opening in the conversation and allowed her at last to have her say. She lit only one lamp in the far corner above the children's bookshelf, and they sat in front of the window whose trailing plants showed glimpses between them of the first harbour lights beginning to sparkle. She had offered him a drink which he refused and she sat pulling at her fingers like somebody waiting to be interviewed.

'Have you – never made a mistake, Ben, at any time in your life?'

He gave his familiar dismissive laugh. 'I've frequently made mistakes as well you know. Perhaps coming home was one of them.'

'Perhaps going away was another,' she said, less unsure now. 'The point is *everybody* makes mistakes and some are irreversible like that poor girl's experiments with drugs, but although my mistake was a very serious one I do think I can reverse it. And you can help me, Ben.'

'Oh really?'

'Well, I think you can anyway. If you will, that is. If you will see me for a moment not as your mother (whose decision a few years ago you have a right perhaps to resent) but as a deeply troubled person coming to you for help. You have a kind heart, Ben. You always had even as a child.' Her charming voice was beginning to woo him now and his resistance suddenly strengthened.

'Say on, Mother, and forget the flattery.'

'Well, try to see it this way. It's a question of what's best for both Denis and me now. Separation has been tried and probably he was as briefly happy with it as I was. It was a necessary spacing of our lives, if you like. The thing was given a three-years trial.' She clearly hadn't finished speaking but he had to get one thing clear.

'Forgive the interruption, Mother. Was this agreed between you – a trial separation?'

'Oh no. Not at all. Nothing so calculated.' He failed to smother the laugh at this and she looked sorrowfully at him in the soft light she had arranged.

'Then I think it's very presumptuous on your part to assume Dad saw it like that.'

'Not in the *beginning*, Ben. But do you not think he may be reviewing the situation just as I am now? He's a stubborn man, as you know. However much he wanted us to be together again he'd never make the first move – never. He has to be helped.'

She looked upset when he laughed again.

'Look, Mother, I'd like to save you from making a fool of yourself if I can. You made your own life after the break-up and you made at least one good new friend, my employer, who now wants you to live with him. What has suddenly gone wrong with a life-style that seems to have progressed logically from the moment you nagged my father into putting the house up for sale?'

'I'm ignoring your language for the moment, Ben.'

'That's much the wisest thing to do if you want us to go on talking. What has you so dissatisfied now? What's gone wrong?'

'Nothing. Nothing whatever. Can't you see that Stephen's

wishing to become closely involved has made me consider the clear options for the first time?'

'What are the clear options, Mother?'

'To involve myself again in a full-scale public extra-marital affair and thereby burn my boats and hurt your father or to resume life with him again which would be by far the best thing for both of us.'

She covered her face with her hands and each ear with one finger when he began laughing loudly again.

'Sweet suffering Jesus, if this were farce the audience couldn't be got to believe a word of it! Look, Mother, you have *not* got two clear options – or rather, you have. They are these: do you go on living alone or do you team up with Stephen? *They* are your clear options, believe me.'

'You don't understand, Ben. The very idea of living with somebody else has suddenly made me realise how much I miss your father and how wonderful it would be if things were exactly as they were again.'

'Things can never be exactly as they were again. You tore the home you built together apart, sorted it out into possessions to be divided and four walls to be sold. You did it brutally and deliberately, cold bitch that you are, and now you want to put Humpty Dumpty together again with my help. *No!*' He hadn't intended to lose his temper but there it was.

Her face was still hidden, her ears closed by each of her little fingers, but he knew she heard him. Quite suddenly she dropped her hands and faced him again, the blue eyes swimming in tears.

'You don't think of *him* at all, do you? Of how happy he was here with us all on his birthday. Of how lonely he must be without us still.'

'All right, Mother. You need the truth now and you'll have it. Denis is *not* lonely and you would probably not believe even if you were shown it how well he has managed his own life without you.'

'He has his cats, I suppose,' she smiled in another attempt to charm him.

'Indeed he has. And he also has the company whenever he chooses of an extremely attractive young woman who is in love with him and will probably move in with him any time now.'

'Denis?' The voice was attractive no longer, almost a screech now. 'You're trying to tell me Denis has taken a mistress to get his own back? It's impossible – I know him.' She was walking around now, glaring at him. 'How dare you make up a crazy story like this just to hurt me. Just to try to stop me from doing what I know is right for both of us.'

Ben was laughing again, but biting one thumb and already half-sorry.

'I tried *not* to hurt you, Mother, but you barged ahead, and it was unavoidable. Let me tell you now that your language is a little out of date and you should revise it. Nobody "takes a mistress" any more. People fancy one another and have it off together if and when they please. The young woman I mentioned and my father have been lovers I gather for quite a while now – a year probably. As I said, she loves him.'

'How old is she?'

'Aye, there's the rub, Mother. There's the rub. Twenty-two, I think.'

'It's – disgusting, obscene with a man of his age. I simply can't believe it.'

'You may not Mother. I know her, you see, and I'm happy for him.'

She was white-faced now and so angry that he knew it was only a matter of time before it turned on himself. He got up to go.

'Thanks for –'

'Don't you *dare* get up and go after you've torn me into *pieces*. Asking me to believe that he would take in a trollop off the streets.'

153

'Listen, Mother!' He caught her wrist roughly at last and spoke down coldly into her face. '*That* phrase is rather out of date too, but even eighty years ago it wouldn't have been true. The girl who loves my father is a qualified social worker quite fit to sit at your table or at his, and as I can't tell you often enough, she loves him.'

'Does he love her?' The tone was considerably quieter.

'I honestly don't know. They behave together now like old friends who know one another very well.'

'How do you *know* all this?'

'Never mind, Mother. Look, I know this was a shock for you. But if you think about it, you'll see there's nothing strange about it at all. If *you* want him back after all those years can you not see how somebody else could fall in love with him just for himself alone, for what he is?'

She was crying quietly now, and he knew it was time to go.

'Good night, Mother.'

'Good night. Shall I still see you next week?' She spoke, muffled, through her tears.

'Of course. Maybe before!'

The thing he found worrying as he walked to the railway station was that he had actually enjoyed opening her eyes at last. It was, after all, his home she had torn apart too. Sometimes in vivid dreams he was back there. Everywhere he had lived in Europe there would come some crazy unexpected morning when he'd wake up and reach for the switch of the globe above his old bed again.

15

The cats didn't know it yet but this was the night of their triumph. They did know something was different because Denis was stroking them more than usual and chuckling and seeming to promise them more than the brush cupboard. But the brush cupboard was their lot all the same just as on every other Friday evening. He regretfully closed the door on their glaring golden eyes and then he set his flat to rights. The meal was warming in the oven – cannelloni this evening, and he had six different kinds of salad set out in little bowls. At the last reckless moment he had bought a bunch of pink roses and they were already drooping over the tablecloth in the heat of the evening. He opened the window a bit more and a moth flew in, an oak moth coloured like a particular kind of tortoiseshell cat, and he watched it circle and settle on the tablecloth, on the roses, finally on a spill of light at the window-ledge. He wondered if he should put it out because it would shortly be in danger from the candles but he decided to leave it another while because he liked to look at its vibrating wings, the velvety surface of its body. He remembered suddenly watching a thick cloud of moths arriving every evening when the lights were lit and reflected in the picture windows of a holiday house in Wexford they had rented once. It was a little like looking into an aquarium except that the fish all had wings and were all the colours of the rainbow. They never seemed to realise they couldn't get in. They beat their wings against the glass all night, so that each morning he half expected to find dead bodies spotting the glass, but they were always gone, to reappear again at lighting-up time that evening. He had once carried wakeful Ben out from his room to see the show and the child had fallen asleep watching it.

The doorbell rang before he had quite pulled himself out of his memories and there was Anita to draw him firmly into the present. She was wearing a cotton dress of deep yellow and her skin was brown and warm as she wound her arms around his neck and hugged him closely.

'I love you, Honey Bear.' She kissed him.

'You look very lovely, my dear,' he said, holding her at arm's length to admire the sheen of her skin and the gloss of her hair. 'It's good as always to see you.'

'Why are we so formal, Honey Bear?'

'You are not wearing jeans and I have a weakness for girls in their summer dresses.'

'You have a weakness for girls, I should hope,' she corrected, 'wearing everything under the sun and also nothing at all. Look what I brought you because it's summer at last!' She dived into the wicker bag and held up a punnet of strawberries which she put into his hands and then a bottle of Rosé d'Anjou.

'But why should you bring dessert with you? That's my pleasure and duty surely?'

'It's summer!' Anita said again. 'We can do anything afterwards. We can go swimming after midnight with no clothes on when we have a whole beach to ourselves and we can put your Muscadet into the car and drink it afterwards. It's summer, Honey Bear!'

He shivered.

'Too cold for me even in the daytime, Anita. I'm an old crock you see. It's summer and time for you to find a young fellow your own age, isn't it?'

He spoke with calculated levity, but he watched her shuddering away from the idea.

'Ugh – what do you think? Anybody my age can have a young fellow and welcome so far as I'm concerned. What I

156

have is a better bargain and I'm keeping him.' She hugged him again, then kissed him seriously as though sipping wine, and then again as though she were drinking him.

'Come and eat your dinner,' he said abruptly. 'You must be starving, child.'

She lit the candles while he went to the oven and when he came back she was at the window releasing the moth from cupped hands.

'Now I suppose we must keep it closed or the poor fool will come back to do himself in,' she said, pulling down the sash before sitting down opposite him. She toasted 'To us, Denis' in the rosé wine which she had obviously taken straight out of her fridge before coming here, and he looked at the young glitter of her again across the candles and marvelled at what he proposed to do.

'This food is super,' she said as usual, and then she began to tell him about how well Ben was getting along with the swimming pool. She had seen it a few days ago in the last stages of completion with the help of the young ANCO people and the grant.

'I believe you were instrumental in helping there, Ben tells me?'

'Fortunately my report went to the right bossman who has a special interest in the Gardiner Street area. He cut all the red tape that would have held up the project, pointing out, I believe, that swimming pools are chiefly in demand during the summer and it could be roofed over and better facilities added next September. The basic pool will be ready as soon as Ben hoped it would be, to remain open during the summer holidays. He even has a caretaker willing to take responsibility.'

'Wonderful!'

The conversation died several times after this and he knew it was his fault. She insisted on going to the kitchen then to prepare the strawberries, adding to them the baby brandy bottle she had also taken from the wicker bag. She returned still smiling at him, his cut-glass bowl of strawberries in one hand and in the other a single huge berry dipped in brandy (she said) frostily coated with sugar and held by its stalk between tiny fingers. She left the bowl between the candles and conveyed the berry to his mouth, opening hers as though he were an infant before he caught it in his teeth. She was back in the kitchen whipping cream then as he uneasily put on a record, Peter Skellern singing 'These Foolish Things'.

'I love it,' she said, 'love all those oldies: "Smoke Gets in Your Eyes", "Manhattan", "What'll I do?", "If I had a Talking Picture of you".'

'I remember them first time round, Anita. They weren't nostalgia then. They were the latest hits. I well remember as a child hearing grown-ups discussing the miracle of "the talkies". That's how old I am!'

'What *is* all this?' Anita wanted to know. 'It's a gorgeous summer's night and it's nearly June and here we are eating the first strawberries of the year and we have the whole night before us and you're drooling on about old age. Age is relative. You're not old if I who am young don't think you are. I think you are the dishiest man I know and I'll prove it to you. Now stop it, Denis.' In silence he ate his strawberries and a warm brown hand came across the table and covered his cold one. 'What's wrong, tell me?'

'Nothing,' he said, 'and everything, my dear. We have to talk about it!'

'Not tonight,' she pleaded. 'I just want to love you tonight. Nothing more.'

'Please try to understand.'

'I'll try hard – later. Just eat up your strawberries and finish your wine. We'll forget about the midnight swim and just open your window to the light that's left and be no danger to the moths. I'll show you how little you have to think about old age or anything else when you have me.' She squeezed his hand, came around and sat on his lap and felt his remoteness from this evening and from her.

'Something *is* wrong, Honey Bear,' she said. 'What is it? Tell me, love.'

'I'm tired,' he said. 'I've been feeling for some time that it's you and Ben should be together, not you and I.'

'What gave you this idea?' She sounded anxious now.

'Nobody. It's only a feeling. But it's strong.'

'Look, Denis, I like Ben because he's a nice fellow and your son, but he hasn't the slightest interest in me, nor have I in him.'

'The country is full of young men you could be interested in, and *should* be,' Denis said. 'This fantasy with me is holding you back. I'm the father you tragically lost and I can go on being him to you. But I think we fool ourselves believing that this – little fantasy can go on for ever. Won't you try to understand?'

'We can have a holiday together,' she said. 'I have two weeks at the end of June and more in September. We'll take the ferry and drive down through France to Provence and I can show you the first bit of France I ever saw as an au pair. All right. We can forget that and go to Greece. I know somebody who will lend us a house on Paros. I was going to suggest a holiday tonight anyhow and I don't care where. Anywhere, Denis.'

'I can't go away with you, Anita,' he said gently. 'My travelling days are over. I like routine, I hate disruption. Don't you see it's the very opposite to being young? There's nothing I'd hate more than going away with you and if I ignored this conviction and went you'd have a miserable time too. Forget it, child.'

'You're tired of me, Denis.' Her voice was so small now that he was smitten by it.

'I'm tired of me,' he said. 'Me in the ridiculous role of lover. Congreve wrote good plays about the pretentions of old men like me. Sheridan wrote his best play about me only he called

159

me Sir Peter Teazle. An old man with a young wife or mistress whom he can't satisfy has been the butt of wits for centuries.'

'I love you – doesn't it mean anything to you?'

He stroked her hair as a father might. 'On the contrary it means the most exciting thing that's happened to me since I got married. I am not Lord Byron as I told you before. Nor was meant to be. I can't watch this astonishing and beautiful year come to pieces *slowly* before my eyes. You'd end up as dull as I am and you were made for delight. Try to understand, my dear child. Give yourself a chance now that the summer is just beginning.'

'Give me one more try,' Anita pleaded. 'Just give me this one holiday with you and then if it fails that's it. We won't go away at all. We'll stay here. I'll take the car and we'll find the most remote corner of the west away from luxurious farmhouses and Ryan's hotels. I know beaches we can have to ourselves west of Mulrany. I know corners of that coast nobody else knows. I worked there after my training was finished. I'll show you forgotten bits of the coastline you won't believe until you see them. I know a converted lighthouse we could have for a week if I just made a phone call. Why not just a week, love? Don't, *don't* refuse me this!'

Her head was burrowed into his shirt and he kissed it, leaving his face buried for a moment in its young fragrance.

'I can't go away even for a week,' he said at last.

'You mean you won't. Why don't you just say that and have done with it.'

'I mean I can't.' He got up abruptly and left the table and she heard him snapping a door open. Then before him into the room rushed two huge and menacing cats, eyes glaring, tails expanding. One of them bounded onto her lap and she screamed and went on screaming trying to brush the terrible thing off her but it clung with savage claws that broke through her yellow dress and tore into her flesh. Even as she screamed she could feel the blood trickling between her legs when the terrible creature unhooked her and (no doubt frightened of the noise) bounded into a corner of the room where its owl eyes glowed like lamps fixed on her. It was joined by the other monster after a word from Denis and then he was trying in his treachery to comfort her and stop the trembling. When she finally stopped screaming a storm of weeping followed and she pushed him away in fury. Even although she knew her legs wouldn't hold her up yet she wouldn't let him touch her, but said through the fingers clenched in front of her face:

'Get them away, you scheming treacherous bastard. Just get those killers away so that I can go in peace.'

When she opened her eyes the terrible creatures were gone, but the air smelled rankly of cat and the thought that she had eaten a meal here made her rush to the bathroom where she was violently sick into his hand-basin. She didn't care. Afterwards she ran the tap, splashed cold water again and again over her face, and then, water still dripping from it bent to examine her thighs. They were still trickling blood from three or four deep scratches so she splashed water on them too, drenching her yellow dress and her shoes and the bathroom floor. She didn't care. Her legs were steadier now and she could walk home.

Outside he was repentant, waiting meek as a monk to accompany her but she swerved suddenly to the table and threw a half-full glass of wine into his face before grabbing the wicker bag and running out of the apartment down the stairs and into the grounds where she began to tremble violently all over again, this time in relief. She sat down on the cornerstone of the car park until the trembling stopped, and then she walked quickly through the shrubbery, glad that her own apartment was so near. She knew she would have to find another place soon but that was preferable to seeing him even accidentally ever, ever again.

Two days later, however, she was weeping over his letter, and looking in fright into the empty summer ahead of her.

Dear love,

So I call you for this last time, and so I'll remember you for all the rest of my life. I'll remember your goodness to me and the sweet excitement of loving you. But I'm too old, older I'd say than your own father would be today if he had been spared to you. You were made for happiness, my dear Anita, and happiness I know you'll have with somebody who belongs in your own world. I shall never forget you, but you must forget me as quickly as you can. I was an act of insane generosity on your part. I was an episode and I'm over. Blame it on my decreptitude, my lack of courage, on what are delicately termed my failing powers, which can only fail further, blame it even on my fondness for cats. But I beg you to forgive the suffering which that thoughtless impulse of mine caused you. I wanted to demonstrate to you the difference between us but I had no idea you could be affected as you were. I bitterly blame myself for that. I know how difficult it is for you to believe that poor Caesar was only trying to welcome you when he jumped up on your lap – that is his way with strangers. Mrs Grey, on the other hand, always keeps her distance until she is sure of people. You frightened Caesar when you screamed and that's why he reacted as he did. But two gentler or more affectionate cats never existed. I keep trying to remind myself that to you it is as though you were leapt upon by – say, a large rat. Is that not so, my poor child? That's why I humbly beg your forgiveness and indeed also for the deception of hiding the cats away every time you came.

So my dear Anita, there you have one of so many differences between us. The miracle is that we loved one another despite them for so long. But be loved now as you deserve, my dearest girl, and be happy as you have made me even in this afterglow of our time together.

Ever your friend whenever you need me, Denis.

16

There were many suggestions from time to time that Olivia should visit St Domenic's and she didn't quite know why she had never taken any of them up.

Towards the middle of June, however, she had a letter from Stephen Lydon asking if she would like to attend the official opening of the swimming pool which would be garnished with a couple of government ministers because of the ANCO help the school had received. If not, perhaps she would drop in later that day – June 15th – and have coffee with him in the office and he would show her around.

Olivia's interest was minimal but she went anyhow although her instinct would have been to get out of the city on such a day. It was probably more than a decade since she had been anywhere near this part of the city and she was appalled at what had happened to it. She found it inconceivable that anybody could choose to live and work among such devastation. Working here she could understand since jobs were scarce, but that Ben could choose to live here instead of in her beautiful home which was also his whenever he pleased was something too baffling to brood over. If anything, the hot bright light of midsummer made everything worse. There was nothing to hide the squalor of derelict houses or the demolished buildings whose sites were closed off from trespassers by hoardings. Behind the hoardings a gaunt chimney-stack on the wall where old staircases had once climbed still hung suspended against the blue sky and the hoardings themselves were filthy, covered in obscenities. A smell of urine and vomit pervaded the place but the children playing in the odd green space on swings provided by Dublin Corporation were clean in their summer clothes, screaming and happy as children anywhere. She stopped to watch one such small playground with the extraordinarily young mothers sitting around smoking and gossiping, all of them with prams and toddlers too small to go on the swings. She looked beyond the demolished buildings to the grim box-like apartments where most of them lived and she remembered the stories, half-read and laid aside in her newspaper, of child deaths here from heroin and glue sniffing. This would also be the area, she presumed, where so-called 'joy' riding in stolen cars and the mugging of old-age pensioners would be the weekend recreation of children who had played beside their mothers in parks like these not so long ago. Olivia couldn't imagine what had happened to the contented poor of her childhood, to the civil barefoot children who had sold newspapers in the street, the organ-grinders and the rag-and-bone men, and the decent men and women who often came from the slums to work in good southside houses or gardens and who were spotlessly clean and honest as the day, capable of rearing large law-abiding families on a few shillings a week. She was inclined to think that social welfare benefits were the beginning of the rot, when people began to get the idea that it was quite possible to live without working, and live just as well.

She had left her car in a safe place on the other side of the river (everybody knew it was insanity to park this side) and she walked the few remaining streets to St Domenic's with a quickened pace in the hot sunshine, not wanting to stroll among such squalor for any longer than was necessary. Large ministerial cars had already arrived and the security men were watchful. The official opening was to be at two o'clock. Suddenly Stephen Lydon was coming smiling to meet her, hand outstretched, and she walked with him across a tidy playground to where a platform was erected and yellow ribbons closed off the entrance to the pool. It seemed the whole school was assembled. Ben came briefly to say hello before returning to stand with his students, as tough-looking a lot as could be imagined, Olivia judged. The Headmaster handed her into a place on the platform before he joined the Minister, the security men, the parish priest and the school Board sitting in front. The sun shone fiercely down as the Minister began to speak, meandering on about the wealth of a nation being its young people, its brave young blood that would carry this little country of ours triumphantly into the twenty-first century, by which time his government would by the grace of God and its own enlightened economic policies have brought an end to the curse of unemployment that had blighted this nation of late because of world recession and the mismanagement of the previous government. The Minister had an unfortunate speech defect that resulted in a slurring of the consonants and a tendency in his listeners to look away lest they embarrass him by watching the flying spume dissipating itself in the sunlight or, worse, spraying the front row. Olivia closed her eyes until he had finished and then after the applause she listened attentively to Stephen's crisp resumé of the events which had led up to the successful funding of this amenity to the whole area. Generous mention was made of Ben's contribution and the great help he had received from his pupils until the government kindly saw its way to allowing the ANCO project to go forward. He wanted to thank everybody concerned but especially the young people who had worked so magnificently to finish the pool in time to be an important amenity for the whole district this summer. He hoped he would have the co-operation of parents and pupils in helping to maintain open-house during the holidays, and that they would all give as much assistance as possible to the caretaker Mr McKay. More applause and the Minister stood up again and walked to the yellow ribbons which he cut with a pair of scissors handed to him. A strange-looking green-haired girl was the first to dive into the pool and then other swimmers followed. All were applauded before the bigwigs including herself adjourned for tea in Stephen's study. It was an affable and (she was glad to note) very brief ceremony before they all got into their cars again and were driven off to resume the affairs of government. Stephen breathed a long sigh and held out his hand to her.

'I kept myself going throughout all that waffle with the thought of seeing you afterwards. It was very good of you to come. Let's escape to the Strawberry Beds and I'll buy you a proper tea, how about that?'

'I'm not sure if I should. I thought I might visit Ben who doesn't live far away.'

'This is Tuesday and I can tell you nobody will make Ben budge from here until five o'clock. He gives extra tuition to a few weak people on Tuesdays.'

'All right then, I'll come.'

'Go and see Ben at the swimming pool, why don't you, and then I'll see you here in half an hour.'

'Very well.' She smiled. Why not? And she'd get a chance to put him off again, with any sort of luck.

The Strawberry Beds was an area she had hardly visited since she was a child. At that time it used to be crowded with families down from the city for the day to eat strawberries and cream. Her grandmother had once told her of the excursions she took as a girl on the large old horse-drawn hackney cabs with crowds of young people all competing for the outside seats when they drove home at last in the warm moonlight wearing only their light muslin dresses with wraps and shawls still folded in the carpet bags they all carried. There used to be singing along the river banks, her grandmother said, and melodeon-playing and it might be the last time they would all be together before they scattered for the summer holidays. Olivia herself remembered the taste of warm strawberries and slightly sour cream under the hot June sunshine and she remembered how many of the little tea-rooms had wooden verandas and chairs set out there so that you could eat and watch the river at the same time. The Strawberry Beds themselves were the small sloping hillsides that caught all the sun. On a bright afternoon you could see the berries glowing red which had ripened since the morning. Coming here was one of the rituals of summer. Now the Strawberry Beds were gone, new bungalows were common instead of the small thatched cottages and the place was mainly patronised by groups of young motor cyclists. Their helmets lined the white railings of the pub they favoured. The place overlooked the Liffey which at this point widened a little and was full of green reflections from trees stooping under the weight of their summer leaves. Stephen parked the car among the bikes and they walked down to the river bank before thinking about tea. Midges vibrated in clouds above the water. It was very warm, and she threw off her jacket.

'This is a treat for me, Olivia,' Stephen Lydon said. 'You've been elusive lately. I had almost given up hope of seeing you again.'

'Never give up hope,' she said flippantly. 'I've been busy with various things. My own life is as demanding in its own way as yours.'

'I wouldn't dream of doubting it. But I thought maybe you would have a little time to think over my suggestion. I feel strongly that throwing in our lot together even on an experimental basis might be the best thing that ever happened to either of us. Later I hope we can talk seriously about the future. There's a lot of our life left yet, with any luck. Why should we waste it alone? There are complications obviously on both sides but I believe they aren't insuperable.' The flies down here by the river were a nuisance and he beat at them uselessly for her before he remembered his pipe. After he had filled it and got it going the flies were suddenly not there any more, and she smiled at him properly for the first time.

'Men, or at least pipe smokers, do have their advantages, I can't deny it.'

'Of course they have. Don't you think you'd like having a man around again? I don't mind where we live, your flat or mine. It would be exactly as you'd prefer.'

'It would have to be mine, of course, if I considered it at all. Yours is let furnished, isn't it?'

'Yes, because I left all the furniture with my wife although quite a lot of it was fancied and bought at auctions by me.'

'That was a nice thing to do,' Olivia said, thinking in some shame of her own calculated divisions. Of course your children are younger. Do you ever miss them?'

'Constantly.'

That was all he would say about that, and they walked on in silence. The rushing sound of the river closed off voices and most of the traffic sounds as well.

'The trouble is,' Olivia said, 'you find it difficult to understand my hesitation because you and your wife were quarrelling all the time. Denis and I hardly said a cross word to one another, ever. I may go back to him again, or rather, he may move in with me which would be the more rational thing to do.'

'I understand.' The euphoria of the day was gone and at last he looked crestfallen.

'Nothing', said Olivia quickly, 'has been decided yet, however. I'm bound to admit there may be some resistance on his part. He's quite stubborn and, to his mind, I did the unthinkable.'

'Why don't we have a holiday together, Olivia? Give you a bit of time to think and also it would give both of us a chance to see how we react to one another's company in long stretches. Naturally you could go wandering off alone with your sketchbook if you felt like it. I also enjoy a little of my own company because I'm surrounded by people all day and every day.'

'Where would we go?'

'Why not Venice? – ever been there?'

'Strangely never, although I wanted to go for my honeymoon. Denis said it was a wet unlucky place and that it would probably sink before we got out of it.'

'It's a city created for commerce and the Arts in equal measure which time and pollution have worn down to pure magic, unique and golden and ghostly, a flower, as they say, of cities and made for lovers. Forgive the purple patch but I dementedly love the place and if Denis has never been wrong in his life before he was wrong about Venice. Come with me and see. I know a pensione on the Giudecca Canal which has a matchlessly beautiful setting and isn't even expensive. Come in late June and see how wrong Denis was.'

'Really, you'll have to give me some time – say, even until the end of this month.'

'Done.' Brisk now that he had hopes of a decision, he set capably about entertaining her.

17

Olivia had never visited Denis's home before and she wasn't at all sure she ought to do so now, particularly on this Friday evening. But when she felt unsure and undefended her only remedy had always been action of some sort. She had never suffered in silence in her life. Ben had failed her, and no doubt he had his reasons, but she still had all her old responses intact in a changed situation and she knew what she must do. Confront what was troubling her. Attempt to reverse a mistake once she had recognised it as such.

Even coming to this district had been the first difficulty she'd had to overcome. Since selling the house, she had never seen it or wanted to see it again. But now she decided to buy a little time by walking around in the direction of her old home. There was no actual need to walk up the avenue of early Victorian houses if she didn't want to face it. She would look at the big lime tree and perhaps even smell its fading blossoms, that might be sufficient. But in the end it wasn't possible to resist walking up to the house which, she could see from the distance, had a large tip drawn up outside it. It turned out to be full of torn-out wood and rubble, partly from the old gate and the garden wall which had been demolished to make way no doubt for a car park. The tree in sumptuous bloom had a large black cross on it and she didn't like to speculate about what that might mean. A JCB had been left by the workmen drawn up against the side wall, and the gravel was churned up along its track. The plain arched doorway was gone and in its place the beginnings of a square construction that might be on its way to being a porch with windows like portholes. Behind the chimney-stacks a strange and hideous addition was in progress, no doubt to provide three or four one-bedroomed flats for the young. It would obviously rise a storey higher than the house and its horrific appearance from the avenue could best be imagined. With any luck, Olivia thought, the present owners would be compelled by the planning authorities to bring down the level, but anyhow she wasn't disposed to worry about it. She just hoped Denis would be preserved from the sight of it as she walked hurriedly by, glad there was no sign of an old neighbour around to condemn her.

When she arrived at last outside the apartment block she hesitated only a moment before pressing the bell with her husband's name on it. His voice answered immediately through the sound system. 'Who is it?'

'This is Olivia, Denis.'

She could hear the sudden indrawn breath and his hesitation seemed to last fully a minute. She knew this was nonsense, of course. 'Do come up,' his voice said at last, 'fourth floor' – and the hall door opened automatically. She knew at first glance she could never live in a place like this with its hideous predictability, its tubs of plastic plants in the hall, its fluorescent lighting blocks in the ceiling, its total lack of character. If Denis could be got to see reason it would be very much to his advantage. He was waiting for her at the lift exit and he didn't flinch when she kissed him. He even gave her a formal peck in return before ushering her along the corridor to his door. Inside everything was quite different, a warm colour scheme, a vase of roses mixed with purple irises and a nice smell of dinner. And of course the cats. She bent immediately and scooped up Mrs Grey (always her favourite) who scarfed herself around Olivia's neck and feathered her face with the wonderful tail.

'Come and sit down,' Denis said, smiling at the cat, especially when Caesar jumped up too onto Olivia's lap, not wishing to be outdone by the grey.

'I know I shouldn't have come,' she began, 'and that it's appallingly bad manners not to have phoned you first but –'

'Don't apologise,' he said. 'Would you like a drink?'

'I'll have a sherry, please,' she said meekly, and as he poured it she praised the order of his living-room and how elegant his table set for one looked.

'Would you like to join me? The delicatessen helpings are generous.'

'No thanks, I had a very late lunch, and can't stay long. Coming out here to see you was just an impulse. I hope you'll forgive me?'

'Of course.'

With the slightly baffled look she remembered, he sat down across the room from her and asked kindly, 'How have you been?'

'Very well, thanks. It's just – well, sometimes I find myself remembering things best forgotten and I wonder if we could ever, well, perhaps occasionally for old time's sake meet and maybe have a meal together or go to a concert in the NCH. I've been thinking about phoning you for so long and never doing it that I decided I'd take myself as well as you by surprise this evening because I have tickets for the Brahms Night on Sunday and –'

'It's extremely kind of you Olivia.' He paused and with an experienced hand she lifted down a cat and buried her nose in its fur to hide her anxiety.

'Mrs Grey always smelled of the very *best* shampoo,' she said. 'How does she do it?'

'She likes bathrooms, don't you remember?'

'Yes, of course. That *was* Mrs Grey. She's handsomer than ever and looks no older. Nor do you, as a matter of fact.'

'There's nothing to age us,' Denis said. 'It's a very soft life here and entirely pleasant.'

'People who say men can't live properly alone ought to just *see* the neatness of this flat when one just walks in off the street. It's lovely. Maybe, though, it's a little lonely at times?'

'Not a bit. I have the bad taste to enjoy my own company in addition to that of the cats. Let me freshen that for you.'

'Just a smidgin' then.'

He topped up the dry sherry and she saw he didn't want to be rude. 'Your suggestion for Sunday night, I must say, sounds very nice. I'll come.'

'Wonderful.'

She set down the cats, who instantly moved to Denis's lap and ran along his arms when he outstretched them.

'I do remember your circus act,' she said.

'It's not my act, it's theirs. They taught it to me, as cats tend to do. That's why it's difficult to teach them conventional tricks.'

'Maybe what I need is a cat,' she said suddenly.

'It was certainly very generous of you to let me have them both. Time perhaps I bought you another. Your birthday is coming up next month. How about a sealpoint Siamese, or would you rather be surprised?'

'I'd rather be surprised.' She was so happy that she decided to go soon before anything spoiled this visit. She finished the sherry as they chatted a bit about the family and especially about how well Ben was doing. Denis heard with a smile the story of the swimming pool and its official opening and then she made an excuse about having to be somewhere in town.

'I'll see you down,' he said, and later waved to her from the front entrance. They were to meet at the concert hall on Sunday and she went home delighted with herself.

He had no sooner gone back upstairs than Anita phoned. He knew it was she even before he lifted the receiver and he took a deep breath before answering. She, it seems, was just losing what breath she had. He heard the gulp of air, and repeated his hello to give her time to recover. When she spoke at last it was in a very casual tone.

'I just wondered how you were and what you are doing.'

'I've just had an unexpected visitor and I'm a bit late with dinner. I'm very well, and how are you?'

'I'll survive,' she said. 'That letter will help. Thank you. I can't answer it at the moment but maybe some time I will. First I want to say I'm sorry for the things I said. For the hysteria too. I came to a bad end, after all.' She could hear his small laugh and it cheered her. 'Don't think of me like that, will you, Honey Bear?'

'Never. I told you how I shall think of you, with gratitude always and a little sadness that you were not born earlier or I later.'

'I suppose it's too soon to see you again? Like Sunday evening at my place. I'm cooking dinner for a couple of friends. You would bring us up to four which is a nice number. Would you, Denis?'

'I'm truthfully not free on Sunday evening. But even if I were I think it's much too soon. You must give us both time to get used to living without the boost of one another's company. Otherwise there will be more unhappiness for us both. Try to understand, Anita.'

'I'm trying. But I'd rather be miserable after seeing you than despairing without you. Can't *you* understand.'

'I can but a period of unhappiness, even desperation if you want to be dramatic, is inevitable and necessary. When it's over we can be friends, happily meeting occasionally.'

'When will it be over? When will my legs stop shaking when I'm speaking to you on the phone? When will your voice stop sounding inside my head when I'm at work? And when will every bump and hollow of your body stop haunting the tips of my fingers? When, Denis?'

'In about three months', he said, 'at most. And probably

174

much sooner. I can remember feeling that way about people before, and so can you. You don't believe it will fade, but when you use your memory you *know* it will. Just be patient and don't refuse any invitation to join any young people you know, especially at weekends. You've already made a sensible beginning for Sunday by inviting friends in.'

'Only because I thought you'd join us,' she said catching her breath and abruptly rang off. With no effort of the imagination he saw her fountaining tears, her body flung down on her bed with face pressed into the pillow. Poor child, he truly had a lot to answer for. Dinner forgotten, he sat down and wrote her another letter.

18

The hot June days before the end of term were full of examination trauma for some and for others full of the joys of swimming. An instructor had been engaged one day a week by the headmaster and he took relays of non-swimmers who were not sitting for exams all day. Ben watched for a letter with the expected Dutch stamp and was disappointed but otherwise very satisfied. He had made up his mind to go to Holland for a couple of months anyhow and find somebody to live in his flat. He thought it wouldn't be difficult. Even if Julie did not write to him, tracking down an Irish girl who was cataloguing the library of a Mr Tappe in Haarlem should be quite easy. The more he thought about Holland, the more it appealed to him as a summer venture. It had been his first taste of liberty during college days, his first acquaintance with the pragmatic Dutch whose honesty in personal relationships appealed to him. He could never forget the symbolic ties between his impecunious bunch of layabouts and the solid burghers of Delft, the careful sorting out of the cast-off domestic equipment and furniture into material for the garbage man and offerings for the squatting Irish students to be left diplomatically on the little leafy courtyard off which their rooms opened. That was the way those rooms had been furnished to a standard of comfort amazing to the frequent newcomers from Ireland. He supposed all that squatting of the mid-seventies was over now, but the same tolerant attitude to transitory guests of the nation probably remained. He would enjoy the order, the beauty and the thrift of Holland again, the Dutch refusal to go fascist as an easy option amid the growing violence of Europe.

As for Julie, he had seen her grow from dangerous and terrified immaturity into as nearly a junkie as made no difference, and from that into somebody who was prepared to come to terms with her own limitations. He began to think that perhaps with him her best chance of total reclamation lay and that in her he would finally find the basis of his future life. He no longer viewed marriage or an alternative long-term commitment as potential shipwreck. He actually thought without flinching of parenthood, if ever she wanted it. Perhaps, of course, he fooled himself. It was only by going to Holland he could find out, so he booked a flight to Amsterdam for July 1st and felt very happy about it.

On the day the school broke up he got a letter which made him blink and re-read it in delight, although in truth the combination of block capitals and inelegant caligraphy was a mess. But its message was clear and even on the second reading a huge smile spread all over his face.

Dear Sir,

I kem to tel you we were of to Rosnowla for the holdays befor the last day off school butt you wernt in the clasroom. I can rede a bit and now you see I can rite so thanks. I will be bac to school in Septembre. I tole Mr. Nolan in Dorsett Street.

Pauline.

By God, Pat Nolan had done a good job and he lifted the staff-room phone to thank him. He thought of that abused slum child happy on a Donegal beach with her foster family obviously determined to come back to school and he knew if he was a praying man he would go down on his knees this minute in gratitude. Instead, after he had applauded his friend he went to the headmaster's study and knocked at the door.

'Well, Ben. Are you all set for the holidays?' They chatted for a few minutes about plans – Stephen, it seemed, was going alone to Venice – and Ben was touched by the fact that he had never been pressurised by this man about whether or not he was returning in September. The time for decision had really been weeks ago. Ben watched the question now forming in his mind as Stephen knocked out his pipe and started the process of refilling.

'You'll naturally want to know whether or not I'm coming back and I must apologise for leaving it hanging for so long.'

'I fully understand, Ben. We're not offering you a rose garden as I said before. I'll never cease to be grateful for the unbelievable change you've brought about in this school in a few months. If you've had enough and want to further your own career in a more likely place, I'll still be grateful to you, it goes without saying.'

'I want to stay on, Stephen, if it's OK with you. As I told you, I never expected to come home to a rose garden – not my line, really. Here I get what I suppose the sociologists mean by job satisfaction. I'm not throwing it away now that I've been lucky enough to get a taste of it.'

'Thanks be to the Almighty God!' the headmaster said fervently, and went to fetch a bottle of Black Bush from his cupboard. They drank to next September and, unbidden, Stephen began to fill Ben in on his mother. He had invited her to spend a couple of weeks in Venice with him but she hadn't been able to accept. He had to respect her reasons. Ben sighed.

'She's holding out for my father again,' he said, 'and she's lost that one already. If I've ever had a strong instinct about anything, this is it!'

'I must not push her, Ben, although I can't deny I'm disappointed about the holidays. Who knows? I may win by being patient if your hunch is right. Although *of course* this is presumption on my part. Olivia would suit me far better than I her and I have a feeling she knows it. Also, of course, you could be wrong about your father.'

'Good luck to you either way,' Ben said, shaking hands with this disciplined man whom he had grown to respect.

A few days before he was due to fly out to Amsterdam he dropped over to Alison's house, and only remembered on her doorstep that she had been adamant about being phoned before he called on her. Expecting a cool reception then, he was surprised by her warmth. She kissed him and drew him into her dolls' house and then at once set about making him coffee. Her work was lying about on the table but she brushed it aside and took him first, as he requested, to see his nephew, fallen asleep in his playpen under the apple tree. On her way back to the coffee-making, she snatched up a newspaper from a chair in the patio and left him with a remark thrown back over her shoulder about how happy young Olivia was at play-school.

Ben sat contentedly sniffing in the freshly roasted coffee until she reappeared with dark blue pottery mugs and a matching jug from which she poured immediately.

'You haven't seen the papers yet this morning, Ben?'

'Not yet. I usually get around to them over lunch, but I just might have looked at yours if you hadn't needed it urgently elsewhere. Anything new?'

'Not really,' she said quickly, and then brushed the subject away to replace it with her summer plans. They were taking the children for two weeks to a cottage near Clifden and then she and Colm would have a week at least together in Holland from which they hoped to bring home a sturdy uncomplicated Dutch girl to replace poor Monique.

'Holland?' said Ben happily. 'I just might see you there,' and he told her of his own plans, mentioning Julie along the way. To his surprise Alison seemed less than interested, rather abstracted in fact, and he began to regret disturbing her at her work. He mentioned their parents then and she brightened, pouring him more coffee, and more for herself.

'Wouldn't it be *wonderful*', Alison said, 'if they could manage to make a go of it again? This affair of Dad's was obviously a flash in the pan as I knew it would have to be, and of course anybody could tell she's not really interested in her amorous headmaster. *That* was just boredom, no doubt.'

'I simply don't understand you,' Ben said, shaking his head. 'Why can't you accept that she *genuinely* wanted a life of her own after all those years of family life? The old man obviously wouldn't have chosen to break up anything, but when it happened I *assure* you he remade a very pleasant life for himself without delay and found somebody to share it with him regularly.'

'That girl!' Alison said impatiently. 'Younger than we are – he's making a fool of himself there and right well you know it!'

'Expressing an opinion like that out of total ignorance of the situation is not like you,' Ben said. 'I happen to know her and she's in love with Denis. It's not a passing affair so far as she's concerned.'

'Let's leave it then,' Alison said, tiredly, as though re-membering something. 'When exactly are you going away, Ben?'

'In two days.'

'Excuse me a minute,' she said then, leaving him for the second time at peace among the dappled green of the patio. In the silence the traffic was a distant humming and for the first time this morning he heard the sound of the river. The child in the playpen began to wake up, and Ben went over to gaze with delight through the bars at the apple-cheeked face with its two square front teeth gleaming at him through the dribbles. Ben was playing finger-games with the baby when Alison came back, a newspaper held open in her shaking hand.

'Ben,' she said gently, brown eyes exactly like her daughter's now and streaming with tears. 'Poor Ben.' She held him while his eyes flicked at once to the short front-page report headed

YOUNG WOMAN FOUND DEAD IN COUNTY DUBLIN

An enquiry will be held to determine the exact circumstances leading to the death of Ms. Julia Blake, aged 26, whose body was found by a friend last night in what local people describe as a 'junkie commune' in Blackrock, Co. Dublin. A post-mortem will be carried out today, but so far Gardai have refused to comment on unconfirmed reports that Ms. Blake died from an overdose of heroin. Her family home is in Monkstown, Co. Dublin . . .

Alison went on holding him when the newspaper fell rustling to the grass and he began to shake, as though in freezing cold. 'Come and sit down, Ben,' she whispered, but he dropped down onto the grass beside the playpen, eyes closed, one hand pressed against his mouth. When he took it away his teeth were chattering, and the baby suddenly began to wail. Alison picked her son up and held Ben with her other arm but he put it gently away, and went away through the house, banging the hall door behind him. In the warm sunshine of the garden Alison and her son went on crying together, the child hugged helplessly in her arms.

Ben never afterwards remembered exactly where he walked that morning. He remembered the sea at intervals, park benches, the sensation of hunger followed always by nausea, and he remembered crowds of people from whom he was trying to get away. He remembered the polished wooden seats of an old church where he took refuge from the worst heat of midday and he even remembered some of the names inscribed on the brass wall plates: 'Brigadier Henry William Thompson, Queen's Own Regiment', 'Ann devoted mother and beloved wife of Arthur Reginald Arnold, S.C.' and 'Bertha, infant daughter of Colonel and Mrs Ryder-Robson to whom the Lord gave and the Lord took away'. He remembered the rough feel of warm stone walls along a harbour, the slap of water against mooring ropes, the taste of salt in his teeth when the wind rose and the tide roughened. Eventually he remembered a hotel lounge somewhere, and whiskey after whiskey and then hunger, food of some sort and then nausea again.

The tears were hot on his face, he remembered, when he stood outside an apartment door near his father's home, but a strange face answered and told him Anita had left a week ago. And then finally he was pressing his father's bell, shaking still but composed, and his father's voice was telling him to come up, and inside the apartment he was crying again, finding friendship at last and an understanding of his catastrophic loss.

19

Denis liked Sundays. He liked the church bells, the sight of children all dressed up, the smell of bacon and eggs and good coffee which his neighbours had time to prepare only at weekends, he liked the folk Mass he attended at the little church up the street. There was a red-haired girl with a piercing sweet voice which hung magically suspended above the others. 'Our Father who art in heaven / Hallowed be Thy Name.' He liked the bold rhythms they beat out, the incorporation of secular songs like 'Morning has Broken' into the liturgy, but most of all he liked the shaking of hands as a sign of peace. The young people of the choir wore ordinary teenage clothes, jeans, jogging shoes, bright check shirts or black batwing affairs and their hair (all but the redheads) was cropped and ugly or dyed into strange primary colours, or long and bleached into the consistency of straw. Only the red-headed girl had a conventional crown of flowing glory that would not have been out of place in a Pre-Raphaelite painting, but the point is they were not drop-outs from religion as were all the other young people he knew, including his own.

He had taught Ben and Alison to think for themselves and when they were grown they had rejected the pieties of their childhood and this was perfectly all right with him. Olivia had in all honesty parted company long ago with the Roman Catholic Church over its repressive sex laws and he respected her for it. But he went his own way, accepted still the frame of worship in which he had been reared and used his own conscience about the rest. He believed this was what he had been given a conscience for and he approached the Communion table with the same confidence as when he had kept the puritanical laws which he believed the early Christian Church would have found surprising. He could find in the Ten Commandments, for instance, no express prohibition of sexual relations outside marriage except in the matter of property rights – 'Thou shalt not covet thy neighbour's wife' – and since the equality of the sexes had long since been recognised, that hardly applied any more. The wife had an accepted right to her own decisions about her own behaviour. Maverick though he was within the fold, Denis was still devoted to the ancient rituals and he also liked their revised form. He left the church every Sunday with the sound of the young folk-group ringing in his ears, at peace with himself and with his neighbours. It would never have occurred to him to reprove his family for their decision not to worship formally on Sundays, but he regretted it all the same. He thought they were missing something.

He was used to the sort of day he had never been able to achieve in the old life, a day that gradually established its own patterns. He walked for an hour or so before breakfast, sometimes along the river, sometimes in the woods, he listened to music over a long, complicated breakfast which began about half-past eleven and often went on until one o'clock. Over it he read the newspapers and, since her trouble with the poor unfortunate little French girl, he had taken to ringing his daughter Alison most Sundays around their lunchtime to see how things were going over there. They invariably invited him to join them for a meal and he sometimes accepted.

This Sunday Alison lingered when the conversation was really over, and she mentioned Ben's tragedy before getting on to the real purpose of the delay.

'I hear you are going to the NCH with Mother tonight.'

'Oh yes, she's invited me.'

'I don't know if you realise how happy it's making her that you are friends again.'

'We've always been friends, Alison,' he said gently.

'Well, let's put it this way, Daddy. She really *does* regret what happened and would like the whole thing reversed.'

'I must confess I think you're mistaken, my dear, wildly mistaken. Our lives have gone their separate ways by your mother's choice and I don't think either of us at this stage would wish to reverse anything. We're quite happy as things are, you see.'

'She's not – I know she's not, because we've discussed it. She wants you back again.' There it was, boldly out at last! He laughed, but not unkindly, at the simplicity of this.

'My dear child, you must allow us to sort out our own lives for ourselves. It really doesn't concern anybody else.'

'You mean I should mind my own business, Daddy?'

'I wouldn't put it quite like that, love. But you must accept that pressure from outside (from however close the quarter) is not helpful at the moment.'

'Will you come over to lunch and we'll talk about it, Colm, you and I? Colm doesn't entirely agree with me.'

'Thank you, but it's not possible for me to get over to you today.'

'We could collect you.'

'No thanks!'

He put down the phone shaking his head at the thought of Alison matchmaking again. The smooth tenor of his Sunday was disturbed, but he didn't blame the child. Her wild oats had been well and truly sown and now she was more middle-aged than himself, he often thought. Back to his own reflections over the last of his coffee again he wondered if he had been very foolish to agree to go tonight. Would Olivia take a simple friendly falling-in with her suggestion as a come-on? He hoped not, but Alison had made him uneasy. As he fed the cats, he half-wished he had refused the invitation, and even wondered if a phone call would be possible now. But that was an act of discourtesy of which he was incapable. He must go to the concert.

In fact, he didn't even like Brahms, apart from the *Requiem*, and he found the whole thing a trial tonight. Olivia had ordered wine for the interval and they threaded their way through acquaintances in the foyer whose faces expressed quick surprise to see them together although nobody commented. He found himself ill at ease and abstracted in conversation. Olivia was animated, knowledgeable about the conductor, critical of the strings, yet the whole mood of this interval was triumphant as though he had committed himself irrevocably by this public appearance with her. During the second part of the concert he reproved himself, rather than listened to the music. Olivia was naturally vivacious, she behaved like this with everybody – how vain and unkind to read any more into it! Yet the thought that he might be right continued to worry him throughout the second half of the concert and caused him to walk in silence with her to the quiet street where she had parked her car. Olivia chatted on, apparently not noticing his unease.

'Now, I could drive you home straightaway,' she said, 'or you could come home with me for a little cold supper. One way or the other I will drive you home.'

'No thanks, Olivia, I live so much nearer town than you – you forget that I'm only a most pleasant twenty-minute walk away on a fine summer's night.'

'But it's precisely because it *is* a fine summer's night that we shouldn't end it so early – do come back with me. It must be ages since you've eaten.'

'I'm not hungry,' he said firmly, 'but thanks very much for the offer and for wanting to drive me home. You *do* remember how apt I am to walk everywhere?'

'Of course, but are you sure?'

'Quite sure, Olivia. Thank you very much for the concert.'

'It could have been better, but never mind, there will be other evenings. By the way – you didn't happen to find any old letters left behind in the davenport, did you?'

'Only one. I've put it aside for you.'

'Oh there's no hurry with it. Good night, Denis.'

Quick to catch his mood she didn't kiss him but squeezed his arm tightly as she thanked him for coming along, and then (as ever) was hardly inside the car when she was driving off. No fumbling with keys or ignition. No trouble with the seat belt. A couple of unhesitating movements and she was gone, and he was walking broodily away, regretful, unhappy, desperately sorry he had not foreseen all this and now absolutely certain that she had left his long-ago letter deliberately for him to find in the drawer. She hadn't changed, but then why should he have thought she had?

Shoulders hunched he walked on past the gaunt new architecture of Harcourt Road and up into the ruins and reassessments of South Richmond Street. Olivia had always agreed to changes and then set about reversing them quietly. She had broken up almost thirty years of marriage on some strong impulse or other, never believing that the pieces couldn't be as easily put together again as an altered rockery in the back garden or a springtime changing about of rooms. The thing was to try to see it from her point of view. She had been free of maternal commitment at last so why not push it a little further and see how total freedom might work out? Not so well apparently. She must have been missing the old routines quite as much as he had in the beginning but very typically she would not say so. She would set quietly and efficiently about undoing the mistake. Poor Olivia. He felt almost like her father as he let himself into the flat, refreshed and resolute after his walk.

My dear Olivia,

Back home again, I want to try to set my thoughts in order for the benefit (I hope) of us both. Forgive any presumption you may detect in this letter, but I feel you may have read a little more into my acceptance of your kind invitation than in fact I intended. To put it baldly I want us always to be friends but I never again envisage our sharing the same roof. Maybe this is because I have become so set in my ways this past couple of years. It makes me wonder whether if I had never encountered your vitality and drive all those years ago I would ever have married at all. Basically I think I've always been a loner who for most of a lifetime gratefully enjoyed the miracle of family life you created and then reverted to formula again. I doubt if I would now be capable of sharing a home with anybody, but least of all with you because I would keep remembering how it all used to be when there were four of us. Had it never been broken I suppose the change would have established itself gradually and we would have grown into dull resigned old people together.

But even as I write these words I know they don't have anything to do with you at all, do they? You are too strong and impatient a creature to accept limitations, even to accept change. I see you going on to make challenges for yourself to face all the days of your life and may it be a long and happy one.

Remember, dear Olivia, the decision to break up was yours and I think it was a wise one. Remember how you felt when you made it and then look forward, not back any more. In that future I have a part, I hope always, because of great affection and family ties but no other part. I'm returning your mislaid letter which I must admit I could not resist reading. How young we were then! Almost it is as if one were reading a familiar work of fiction. It was fact, as we know, and I am grateful for it all. Ever affectionately, Denis.

188

20

The night before he went away on holiday Ben called to see his mother. He found her distracted as she had always been over her own packing. The big windows of her living-room were open wide to the summer night and a fading branch of late lilac nodded almost into the room. Around her was an array of summer dresses, trousers, cotton shirts, books, coloured biros and sketchbooks. In a ring around her as she sat on the floor were seventeen pairs of newly cleaned shoes and sandals and she was standing her hair on end by lifting her fingers through it over and over again.

'Why', she said, as she had always done, 'does anybody ever go away on holidays?'

'Because routines have to be broken or the human race goes mad, like mice on a treadmill.'

'I *need* all these,' she said, 'every last one of them and every one of those shirts and dresses. If I leave even one behind that is the only one I shall want for some nice evening. You were always so good at packing, Ben. Even as a child. I remember so well how you would have your little bundle of clean clothes all neatly rolled up into a sausage while Alison was rampaging around throwing things out and putting them back again. Like me. Help me, Ben?'

'Only if you go and make coffee and leave the clothes part at least to me. How many bags are you bringing?'

'Only one grip – that over there, and a sort of kitbag for my sketching things and books.'

'Very well. I know where you are going and I think I know most of your clothes and what you *really* wear as distinct from what you believe you'll need. I'll help you if you will promise to abide by the bundle I shall roll to my special crease-free formula. OK?'

'OK, Ben. You're a darling.'

She went away and he had to laugh at her. Rigidly organised in everything else, she went mad when it came to packing. Every garment that had been bought for its elegance but never worn went in. She never had enough of the garments she liked to live in and would burden herself with the necessity for washing, almost every holiday that he could remember. He selected three cotton shirts and trousers that would match well, and a couple of silk shirts for covering up which would go with everything. Then he selected two dresses for their capacity to travel well, swimming things and three pairs of shoes. But he also wrapped and put in the grip her strongest open sandals for sightseeing and then he went and looked at her selection of underwear on the couch. As always it might well have belonged to a girl and he had to smile at the frivolity of the garments as he rigidly made his selection there too. She wasn't going to be allowed to go overboard here either. He allowed her only one nightgown, since it would probably be too hot to wear any, and an old silk kimono which could probably fold into a matchbox if necessary. When she came back with the coffee her grip was packed and she started to wail over all the things he had left out.

'You wouldn't wear them – you know that. I've left you room for a nice big swimming towel because they go mad in that demented place if you take away their towels to the beach and from what I know of Venetians they wouldn't think twice of loading the price of a towel onto the bill. By the way, you

190

probably won't want to spend much time swimming but you'd better see the Lido.'

She thanked him and poured his coffee. 'Dear Ben, I can almost certainly trust you. I should know that.'

'Don't dare *touch* that packed grip until you're setting off, mind.'

'All right, Ben. You have absolutely no idea how excited I am about Venice. It's like being young again. Doing this *appalling* rethink and having the nerve to ring up and ask him if he'd mind if I come after all. It was unprincipled, wasn't it?'

'Entirely. But you're at least not leaving Stephen under any illusion about the sort of woman he's getting.'

'You know of course that if –'

'No, stop it, Mother, no tears. What you were asking of my father was totally unrealistic and he let you know in the kindest way he could.'

'He's harder than I am,' she said, sniffing and suddenly pushing away the coffee. 'I couldn't have done it if the positions were reversed.'

'He's not hard, he's logical, Mother, and I think we'll stop talking about him now, because you'll push yourself into recriminations again. You'll have a wonderful holiday and you'll quite likely discover that Stephen can be lived with very easily afterwards.'

'I'm so selfish,' she said, 'in the midst of all this I'd forgotten you. Poor Ben.'

'Don't,' he said, and walked away from her over to the window to get control of his face again. 'I don't want to talk about it – some time perhaps, but not now. I came over to tell you I'm going away as planned tomorrow.'

'To Holland?'

'Yes. I still have friends who are quite as mad as when we were all students over there. A holiday with them is Disneyland so far as I'm concerned. I'm going tomorrow.'

'So you'll take a shower tonight since you haven't got one at home?' She was happy and beaming at him again, the triumphant provider.

'No I won't. I'll take a deep expensive bath from you tonight and I'll probably use a whole bottle of your bubble stuff.'

'Do, love.'

In her bathroom he lay happily soaking for a long time in the shadow of her trailing plants. He had a sense of time suspended, perhaps suspended for the whole summer, but that thought brought him back to his mother again. He remembered that he had failed to provide her with a single woolly garment for the odd cool night in Venice and he leaned over on his elbow and wrote WOOL on the steamy surface of her bathroom window. Then he relaxed completely into the warm bubbles again in which man and child were one.